blueprint

blueprint

Charlotte Kerner

Translated from the German by
Elizabeth D. Crawford

Lerner Publications Company ■ Minneapolis

This American edition published in 2000 by Lerner Publications Company

Lerner Publications Company
A division of Lerner Publishing Group
241 First Avenue North
Minneapolis, Minnesota 55401 U.S.A.

Website address: www.lernerbooks.com

Library of Congress Cataloging-in-Publication Data

Kerner, Charlotte.
   [Blaupause. English]
   Blueprint / by Charlotte Kerner ; translated from the German by Elizabeth D.
Crawford.—American ed.
      p. cm.
   Summary: Siri Sellin, one of the first human clones, writes a bitter memoir of
her childhood as the daughter of a famous and self-absorbed composer.
   ISBN 0-8225-0080-9 (lib. bdg.: alk. paper)
   [1. Cloning—Fiction. 2. Mothers and daughters—Fiction. 3. Musicians—
Fiction. 4. Science fiction.] I. Crawford, Elizabeth D. II. Title.
PZ7.K45787 B1 2000
[Fic]—dc21   00-008150

Manufactured in the United States of America
1 2 3 4 5 6 – BP – 05 04 03 02 01 00

. . . gerade deshalb D.
gewidmet

. . . dedicated to D.
just because
C.K.

for L.W. P.
from E.D.C.

"The animal breeder *knows* what qualities he
is looking for in an animal every time. But do we,
too, know what we want in a human being?"

Hans Jonas, philosopher

Contents

Blueprint:
Prologue

Iris was inconsiderate, so don't expect any thoughtfulness from me. I'm just following in her footsteps.

In a sense I am also cloning myself, as I bring forth my memories and thoughts and assemble myself again. After twenty-two years I'm creating myself anew. For I am a survivor, trying to comprehend: our beginning and end, her end and my beginning.

My mother-twin died two weeks ago, and I'm sitting the way I used to at our black concert grand piano, which seemed so frighteningly powerful to me when I was a child. We named it Mr. Black when I was seven years old and Iris finally allowed me to play on it. I was full of pride then as I stroked the black, shining wood and the white and black keys.

Never again will I strike these keys. The lid remains forever closed, like the coffin in which Iris now lies.

There is blank paper lying on Mr. Black's wooden back. But unlike Iris I do not use the sheets to pen notes on black lines. I compose no music. I only fill the pages letter by

11

letter, word by word.

I intend to find out who this person sitting here at the piano is.

I don't like the word *clone*, by the way, because it's become threadbare and jokey. I prefer to call myself a *blueprint*. A blueprint is a copy that is made without detouring through a negative and displays white lines on a blue ground.

Blue has always been my favorite color and, of course, was also that of Iris, that arrogant woman who considered herself a goddess. My story, which I shall call *Blueprint*, just like myself, began in the year zero, when I was created and born.

Double Goddess
The Year Zero

When Iris thought of me for the first time, she was surely feeling just as alone and desperate as I do now. She had MS then, and I've been emotionally ill since she left me. It's terrible to be alone when one is ill. We both know that. And so once again I'm so close to her it hurts.

That I'm one of the first human clones, and, in addition, one of the first of our kind to have grown up and survived, is of course not visible to the naked eye. Externally I appear entirely normal, look and talk like any singleton. The horror goes on internally, where the most effective horror, the invisible kind, takes place. Have you noticed? The person who sings the loudest is often the most afraid.

Basically, what I want to write is just my story of our life: Siri's story. Yet, I am trying to write the truth. And what is "the truth?"

Truth is what Iris told me, or the answers my doctor "father" gave me when I met him later and talked with him.

But first and most important, truth means those things that I remember. So don't expect any normal biography. For truth is also what I experienced as twin sister, as Iris-clone, beyond the facts. And because we always remained one heart and one soul—and maybe even still are—I can slip very easily into Iris's skin and mind. After all, as a clone, I can be Iris or Siri, or I am both of us at the same time. I can also climb out of this person altogether, and then I am some third person telling the story of Iris and Siri. Then I can view myself/her/us like a scientist observing her experimental subjects in the cold, blue light of the laboratory.

Iris had just turned thirty years old when her optic nerve became inflamed for the second time and she had to bury her last hope. There was no longer any doubt: multiple sclerosis was in her body, and the various medical tests confirmed it.

Iris had thoroughly informed herself of the implications of MS. The Sellins always want to know the truth; otherwise they feel powerless. The hard statistics said the disease would probably erupt within ten years. Over time, more and more inflammations, like cable fires, would damage the nerve sheaths and fibers in her body and perhaps ultimately leave her crippled, blind, or even demented. Whatever the course of the disease might be—mild, severe, or malignant—it threatened her, the renowned pianist Iris Sellin, with a relentless decline.

With this second optic nerve inflammation in the summer before the year zero, dark walls moved into her field of vision from each side and formed a black alleyway leading into an abyss. In her dreams, Iris peered into this dark hole, from which there was no way back. But she swore to herself she would not fall. Awake, she pounded her *no* on the keys of the piano until her fingers hurt.

The diagnosis of MS flung her out of the normal world and made her rebellious and defiant. She did not intend to bow to this fate, not she. Never! Night after night she turned sleeplessly in bed and cursed her body, which so miserably failed her. "Why me?" she cried.

Her career, her art, her composing had always been everything to her. But suddenly that didn't count anymore. Suddenly she grieved that she had no children. No one to whom she could pass on her talent, her knowledge. No one who would succeed her. No one in whom she would live on. No one whom she really loved and who would love her in return. Iris had never realized how alone she was. In her deep hopelessness she was overcome by feelings that until then she'd scorned as primitive reproductive instincts.

In this time of despair, she happened on a newspaper article about Professor Mortimer G. Fisher of the Centre for Reproductive Medicine and Bioengineering in Montreal, Canada. At another time she would probably have skipped the article, or at best skimmed it and forgotten it quickly. But what it said electrified her: The English scientist had made the cloning of mammals more certain, for he had finally discovered the long-sought central developmental switch in the gene and could now intentionally "turn it on." After Iris had read the report through several times, she knew what she had to do to change her fate.

Only when things were going badly for you, Iris, only then did you long for a child. You wanted a new life to set against the old, sick one. Out of rage. Because you couldn't believe that a person passes away. You wanted to live on in a new life or, even better, to live forever! A desperate wish that only someone desperate could come up with.

When you read Fisher's report, you thought for the first time of me, your clone-daughter, and this thought never let go of you. It gave your life a new meaning and a new goal: me. Or more precisely, you once more. Iris Sellin the first and the second.

My future mother was not ahead of her time. She was just acting in the spirit of the times, and we clones were on the horizon. The single-parent family at generation was on the societal agenda. For the sexes to be finally entirely independent of each other—immaculate conception for each—what an advance! But caution is needed—with each step into the future comes the danger of tripping and falling, of bruising black and blue.

Iris Sellin acted quickly. Through her manager, Thomas Weber, she informed a concert organizer in Montreal that she unexpectedly had a date free the following month and asked whether there would be any interest in an appearance on such short notice. The assent to a concert in October came promptly. Iris sent Professor Mortimer Fisher two concert tickets (for it was very likely that he was married), third row center. In an accompanying letter she asked for an appointment the following day because of an urgent matter. A short time later, Fisher confirmed the requested appointment.

The next six weeks passed infinitely slowly, but finally Iris Sellin was on stage in Montreal. She found the scientist in the audience without any difficulty, for she already knew what he looked like from his picture in the newspaper. During the final applause she made eye contact and nodded to him.

A press photo from that time shows how my mother looked when she was pregnant with the thought of me. I like the picture because it is so typical of her/me/us—very typical: her face is rather round and not delicate, but she looks attractive and intelligent with her high forehead and firm, aggressive chin. Her large gray-blue eyes look stern and create distance, even when they are smiling. Loose hair, which is longish but not curly, falls over her forehead. Standing up on her head rather shaggy and unruly, it makes her look a little like a defiant, wild child. Her lips are beautifully bowed but rather narrow, and when she isn't smiling, they appear compressed. The smile she is wearing in the photograph is winning and at the same time slightly arrogant.

I look exactly the same today, only a few years younger. But a photograph easily swallows the differences between the early twenties and the early thirties. Now let's throw life into reverse: tear the photo to pieces, chew up the scraps, and swallow them. Mother, into the daughter's stomach! Back then it was the other way around.

The day after her successful Montreal concert, Iris Sellin and Mortimer Fisher sat opposite one another. The doctor's office was on the top floor of the Repro, as his reproduction clinic was known in the city. The window looked out on Mont Royal. The trees had already begun to lose most of their colorful foliage. It was the autumn before the year zero.

The doctor expressed his thanks for the concert tickets and complimented Iris: "I found your interpretations of Mozart in the first half of the concert very refreshing. But I was even more impressed with your own compositions in the second half," he said. "Especially the cycle with the Indian names, which I can never remember. That clear structure is so appealing, that series of five separate pieces for violin, bassoon, double bass, and clarinet, and then finally the combination of all the instruments."

"The title of the piece is *Satya*, which means ritual and law," she explained. "All human actions follow laws, after all—magical, cosmic, or mathematical. My music doesn't arise in the world of pure sound alone. The laws lead me to new forms of expression. You do the same thing when you do research. You uncover connections. You venture into new territories. You even decipher the very smallest of all worlds, the cell nucleus. Great scientists are very often good musicians, or at least music lovers. The two of us have many things in common. You also play the piano very well, I've heard. And I almost studied mathematics and physics—don't laugh. As a schoolgirl I wanted to be a second Madame Curie. I've always followed what happens in the natural sciences with fascination."

The scientist was about forty and more attractive than she had expected. Not large, but sturdily built, and he wore a pair of those modish but not too exaggeratedly small nickel-framed glasses. Certainly he read more than just scientific books.

Mortimer Fisher also found the woman opposite him appealing, with her lively voice and the firm look of her eye. He bent toward her, placed his hand on her arm seemingly casually and yet with discernible intention, and asked, "What can I do for you, Frau Sellin? Why did you want to speak with me?"

Iris told Professor Fisher of her two optic nerve inflammations. "I've already become used to not seeing clearly when I focus on something. When I'm playing from music or composing, when I write down the notes, if I always look just past the point to the right or left, it works quite well. . . . I know exactly what lies ahead of me. I've read up on it and there's no doubt about the diagnosis of MS. If I'm lucky, I still have some healthy years left, but then. . . . " Her voice failed.

She had expected the genuine horror she saw on the face of the scientist, and taking advantage of it she asked, "Will you help me?"

Fisher had not expected this question, but he did not allow his surprise to show. He used his quiet doctor's voice to create distance and so collect himself. "But Frau Sellin, you know as well as I do that neither an effective medication nor gene therapy exists for this disease."

"I know that. But you still can help me . . . " here Iris paused.

Pauses are so terribly important. And Iris always knew how to insert a pause very effectively, not only in her compositions but also in real life. Pauses increase the suspense; they prepare us for the climax.

Fisher was not sure what the great pianist wanted from him. "What can I do that others haven't tried already?" he asked tensely.

When Iris Sellin at last produced her request, it sounded entirely plausible. "Clone me," she demanded more than requested.

To make a human being come to life—to be one of the first who dared do it! Fisher had often dreamed of it. And now, not more than a dozen cloned egg cells were necessary to achieve the goal. His procedure had made cloning more reliable. It was time to demolish the old-fashioned taboo against human clones.

"But I've only cloned mice and cattle with the new method so far." Fisher was making an effort to stay calm. He voiced this weak objection to gain time, and he knew how unconvincing he sounded.

Iris smiled almost patronizingly. "I know, and so now take me," she returned, "a willing, female *Homo sapiens*. After all, mammals are mammals. I have nothing to lose and everything to gain. The same is true for you. I may not have long to live. And I assure you, I have nothing against making the whole matter of your success quite public. After all, I'm accustomed to public appearances. In the end, no one can or will be against us or against the clone . . . you know that as well as I do."

No, Iris, you were not just anyone, but someone special. And everyone yearns for the special something that lifts them out of the masses. Who would object to a second Picasso or a second Mozart? Who would object to a second Clara Schumann, a second Fanny Hensel-Mendelsohn? Of course you would never compare yourself to those very great ones, but you weren't average either. Bravo! people would cry. A new Iris Sellin—that would at least be worthwhile. After all, who wants just dumb mass-market merchandise that isn't worth the effort? This is how you tempted him and seduced him.

You had no moral scruples. Whatever would they be? Why should it be harmful to the dignity of a child to endow her with good genes and avoid the genetic lottery, the accidental? No more duds, bull's-eyes guaranteed! Just seize the opportunity! That's a persuasive argument for cloning, to be able to gratify parental desires with certainty.

The desires of the clone interested you less, but how would you two even know the likes of us or our feelings at all? We weren't there yet, not yet of this world, just chimeras born in sick minds, just fantasies of omnipotence.

Fisher had often pondered whether there was anyone strong enough to have a clone. And now, standing before him, a person who actually wanted to be cloned. A person furnished with the required degree of megalomania, the ideal clone-parent. What reason was there to hesitate? This woman who uttered his most secret thoughts was determined to do anything.

Fisher knew this feeling only too well, the deep conviction and the certain knowledge that it must be so. That this alone was the right way, even if the rest of the world drew back or even considered you crazy. He had often had that same feeling in his work, and in the end it had never betrayed him. It was there when he discovered the gene-switch for the embryonic developmental clock and turned it on in a mammal for the first time. That Iris Sellin was standing here now was fate. They had had to meet.

Fisher dropped a question into the tense silence. "And you don't want to hire a surrogate mother? You want to carry this cloned child yourself?"

"By all means! I'll take the risk of the MS becoming worse. It's fifty-fifty, I know that. But my daughter would have the best possible environment from the very beginning. Of course, we wouldn't be growing at the same time in one womb, like other twins. We would be mother and daughter identical twins."

Don't I have to love you for that alone, Mother? You wanted to have me grow in you and not in a stranger. Risking your life for me. But it was a cool, calculated risk you took, Sister. It wasn't love that brought me into the world. There never was any irrational, crazy, beautiful love—it was only self-interest that got me born. I was your survival strategy.

Your voice certainly became increasingly louder and more determined, and I am seeing exactly how that hard line around your/my mouth deepened, which always makes you/me so ugly.

Ruthlessly you expressed to Fisher what you later said to me often enough, "For me a clone is the only choice. I couldn't bear to waste myself on a talentless child."

No, you never wasted your love, not on any child or any man. You didn't know anyone with whom you wished to have a child. You were not created for a true partnership, at most for a cloneship. Deep in your innermost soul, you felt that was the only thing right for you. You couldn't love anyone else as much as yourself. And it was only to love yourself even more that you wanted me, the clone.

Later, when I reproached you for your selfishness, this overwhelming self-love, you never even defended yourself. "That's right. But I'm no exception in that," you replied, smiling gently. "Everybody looks for themselves in their children. Only, I admit it openly. Basically I wanted only me, from the very beginning, only me." Pointless to argue.

You wanted to have yourself created once again. You thought yourself worthy of being reborn. You wanted to be immortal. After all, only someone with such arrogance would even be able to tolerate seeing her exact image. You didn't imagine you would find it difficult, and that was your great mistake. For in fact we are not so easy to tolerate!

Because you were so ignorant then, you moved very close to Fisher without touching him and said, "Become the father of my daughter! Please clone me!"

Any composer knows how tempting, coaxing tones need to sound, how they can raise gooseflesh and erotic tension. And you actually said it: *father*. What a mockery!

Fisher resisted your human seduction but not the scientific temptation; scientific lust mated with human curiosity. He nodded, and with a brief embrace you two sealed the pact: gods, you two.

In the old myths, the father of twins was always either a god or a demon, while the mother of the twins was frequently thought to be a woman who was unfaithful or possessed or a soothsayer. People always considered the birth of twins something special. As an unnatural sign, it heralded good fortune, but also bad.

But before I could be born as Iris's twin—whether as a sign of good fortune or bad was yet to become clear—I had to be conceived. Fisher later told me exactly how and where my cloned life began.

On the morning of the seventh of January in the year zero, Mortimer G. Fisher personally directed the telemicrosope over the cell in resting phase with both joysticks. The laboratory clock read 10:45. He himself had furnished the denucleated cell with the unadulterated Iris genetic code. He had taken this nucleus from, of all things, a skin cell of Iris Sellin. Using a hair-thin glass cannula, he had then inserted the protein to turn on the life mechanism with the Fisher procedure. The switching genes gave no commands yet, and the cell computer remained mute.

The small dot in the cell resembled a black eye. Crumpled together in this little black dot were the client's one-and-one-half-meter long DNA threads. The little dark thing measured just one hundredth of a millimeter, and yet it contained an entire life's program—a human history written down in hundreds of thousands of bands, also called genes. Each of these powerful gene libraries of life concealed so much, commonplace as well as obscure: the appearance of a person and her temperament, her potentialities, and the way she perceives the world. The certainties and uncertainties. A human being from beginning to end.

This damned resting phase, during which all time stood still, made Fisher nervous. Then finally the cell began to divide. The laboratory clock read 11:00, and Fisher was a witness through the telemicroscope as a second life clock began to tick.

The strands of DNA divided and doubled themselves—the threads of fate untangled, struggled apart, and formed two cell nuclei. No longer a single eye, but a pair of eyes—enlarged on the monitor ten thousand times—now returned his triumphant look.

"Welcome, Iris two," he greeted the new life that one day would be Iris Sellin's daughter. He put the scion into an incubator, where in forty-eight hours it would mature into a sturdy eight-celled organism. Two days later the Iris clone gave a healthy impression under the microscope, with all cells regular and well-proportioned. The clone was ready for transplantation.

Iris waited in an adjoining room. Later, there were two things she remembered very clearly. First, that in the room beside the bed there was a comfortable upholstered chair, in which ordinarily a concerned husband would be sitting and holding his wife's hand. That day the chair remained empty, which gave her a feeling of complete independence. She was entirely on her own.

And then there was the recollection that still made her laugh almost hysterically, of her impregnation as an ordinary, slightly humiliating, jiffy-quick procedure.

For the implantation of the embryo she had to place her heels in stirrups mounted on the right and left sides of the bed. Iris found lying there that way, with her legs angled and spread, a little obscene. And so she kept her eyes closed for what came next. Fisher's gown rustled, his breath was audible behind the surgical mask. A female assistant in a turquoise green gown handed him the flexible plastic tubing in which the embryo floated.

"It may hurt a little," warned Fisher as he inserted the cannula through the mouth of her womb.

There was a small but sharp prick, but then only a cool wetness.

"I'll leave you alone now," said Fisher, and his rubber gloves squeaked as he took them off. He briefly pressed the hand of his patient and left the room. With her eyes still closed, Iris Sellin took her feet out of the stirrups, and the assistant covered her before finally leaving the room too.

Iris turned onto her stomach, pressed her hot face into the cool pillow, and stifled a cry of joy and spontaneous laughter.

You had to laugh aloud with happiness. You felt just the way you did composing when you sensed that you had achieved something new, when you could create something that had never existed before.

With your music you ventured into new worlds. Music should never be merely the art of sound, but also the art of the time, and in very special moments, something for the future, you explained to me later. Whenever composing rules are broken, new pathways open.

And that is exactly what was happening when you became pregnant with me: You had broken the rules, the old rules of humanity. The clone-child is the result of a broken rule.

I was supposed to become a very special composition. But our DNA, that twisted ladder, could only produce twisted harmonies from the beginning. Did you really never hear how dreadfully distorted it all sounded? In this instance your perfect pitch deserted you.

So I was floating around inside you as a clump of cells, and you were looking for a name for your dream-child, this still unborn wunderkind.

"I will call you Siri, my child," you whispered. "There is no more appropriate name for you."

You simply read your own name backwards to find mine. How little effort you made in this hazardous game with unknown stakes and unknown rules.

The game of Clonopoly had begun! Roll the dice and advance your token!

Until that point in time, you singletons had only duplicated humans by means of computer programs. Long-dead actors were resurrected and their digital clones were given roles in new films. Supermodels were fabricated by the dozens in the same way, and with the aid of a special command the beauties could be aged at the touch of a button: Folds deepened in the flawless necks, crow's feet appeared around the eyes. Time-lapse photography turned them into aged women.

Scanners could enter the photographs of dead children into computer systems. Then these boy- or girl-tamagotchis could be seen to grow on the monitor, steered by personality programs that scientists had developed from the children's own genetic codes and the personality profiles of the mother and father. In this way the bereaved parents could at least meet their children on the monitor and see what would have become of them had they lived. Some fathers and mothers pressed the Escape button in horror and turned the picture off.

For me it was no more fun: out of the virtual reality of your brain and into the reality of your womb. The Iris-Siri program contained neither the Exit command nor the Escape button. There was no escape for me. From Iris would come Siri.

I wanted to live, yes, or so it appears. But if I'd known what was waiting for me, I might have decided to abort early and not attach myself to the mucous membranes of your womb.

In the beginning, still invisible and lacking willpower, the child was so peaceful and innocent, more an unreal dream. At night, before falling asleep, Iris would stroke her flat abdomen and assure her future partner, "We have yet to become twins, my little doublet. I was a singleton for much too long. Now I'm so thrilled about you. We'll be a beautiful pair."

Ten days after the embryo transfer, a pregnancy test indicated that copy and original were firmly bound to one another from that point on. Until death should part them.

You called Fisher "my Archangel Gabriel" when he gave you the joyous news. In fact, Gabriel was what the G. in his name stood for. What a coincidence—really fateful!

"Thou art highly favored among women, and blessed shall be the fruit of thy genes, Iris. And behold, in the tenth month of the year zero, thou shalt bear a child." Thus the white-coated angel of the twenty-first century should have announced the modern immaculate conception and not simply said to you, "You are pregnant, Frau Sellin. I offer you my heartfelt congratulations!"

For the genius of modern science has biblical dimensions. It converts the heavenly trinity—is that not, after all, the archetype for all clones?—into earthly duality. Oh, earthly creation, with every man and every woman playing God.

You were equally lofty and alone, even in your presumption: You created a human being in your own image. You were man and woman, mother, father, and sister in one.

You dreamed the foolish dream of immortality. You dreamed I would play your music, lend you my hands when your fingers failed to work.

Perhaps when you conceived me you were really as alone and despairing as I am now. But you were obsessed even more.

You brought your idea of me to life. You composed me like a piece of music. Not with the usual sounds of c, d, e, f, g, a, b, but with A, T, G, C. The base pairs adenine-thymine and guanine-cytosine are our chords of life, programmed gene harmony. These four bases cause the life melody of any human being to sound. Your DNA was the master plan, my DNA only a blueprint. From the model to the copy, I am the blueprint of your genes.

Rip, snip, DNA, rip, snip, DNA.

One is made into two.

But to cut someone in half also means to kill him.

Words do not lie, but people deceive themselves. You, too, were fooling yourself in your pregnant happiness.

Iris Sellin flew back to Germany filled with great expectations. In Frankfurt she changed to a small plane that headed for the regional airport at Lübeck, and when the pregnant Iris again saw the silhouette of the city in which her daughter was to grow up, as always she counted the seven tall church towers with their green copper roofs soaring toward the heavens. For the first time she did not feel hemmed in by the brick-red dollhouses, which had always aroused rebellion in her since she'd moved there four years before. At that time, as the youngest faculty member at the Academy of Music, she had accepted the lectureship in music theory and harmony in order to be financially secure. But meanwhile she'd found it possible to make her living from her concerts and, in particular, from composing.

Now suddenly she was looking at this northern city

with entirely different eyes. She looked with the eyes of the child who could not yet see. It was a good place, a beautiful place to grow up in. Much better than the large cities for which she'd been longing the last few years.

Thomas Weber met Iris's plane. He alone knew of the special wunderkind that was growing within her. She had let him in on her secret because he was her closest confidant and her manager. He'd had to cancel her concert dates, rearrange delivery dates for composition commitments, and turn aside questions with the excuse of "time out because of overwork." He had created the time for her to accomplish this conception. At first he'd tried with all his might to talk her out of having the child, but Iris remained as obstinate as always when she'd decided something.

Iris and Thomas had never been lovers but always just friends. He ran the Classics on Stage agency, and from the beginning he'd encouraged her to play her new music and to compose more. "We already have enough music that sneaks into our consciousness like the drone in the supermarket" was one of his favorite sayings. He was her unerring critic and audience and always the first for whom Iris would play a new composition. Such moments brought them closer together than they could ever have been as lovers.

Thomas had never liked this daughter idea. He realized from the beginning that the child would compete with him for Iris's affection. But, as a good manager, he knew how to deal with her, and so on her arrival he placed a "welcome home" present in her hands.

"Careful, it's fragile!" he said.

Iris unwrapped the object from the rustling tissue paper.

It was a reproduction of a statue of a goddess, a small marble figure that Greek islanders had created more than 3000 years before. From the head of the goddess, who had her arms folded under her breast, grew a second smaller but identical woman. Mother and daughter and double goddess, all in one.

Iris Sellin stroked the cool white stone. "It's the most beautiful present you've ever given me," she said.

The white marble figure is still here. And when I take it in my hand, I actually feel the two of us. You were just as hard and cold, and I, too, am as hard as stone. And if we are dropped, we shatter. When you died you let me drop. And now I am a heap of shards.

Iris Sellin opened the heavy wooden door of her apartment on the ground floor of the large house at the edge of the Old City. In the spacious, turn-of-the-century-style reception room stood her piano, and her extra-long work table was in the room beyond. It was there she wrote out her compositions on great sheets of parchment with pen and ink—an old-fashioned method, counter to the times.

She always went to the piano first when she returned from a trip. But now that she had her daughter in her womb, everything was suddenly different.

She walked all the way down the long hallway and opened the door to the guest room. She would turn this into the baby's room. She could already see it: the crib along the left wall, a set of shelves with colored boxes next to the door. The piano would go there on the right wall, just exactly the kind she'd dreamed of as a child. A piano with old brass candleholders that could be swung back out of the way, and beautifully carved legs. In front of it a round piano stool, upholstered in dark-blue velvet. It could be screwed up and down, and when it turned fast, it was like a carousel ride.

Will blue be Siri's favorite color too? Iris asked herself. Will I pass along all my experience to Siri?

Our happiest time must have been our pregnancy. No wonder. I was not yet a human being with a will, only an ideal. While I was growing within you, Mother-Sister, I actually drove out your thoughts of MS. The fear of suffering a flare, the fear of deteriorating physically grew smaller with every day, and I grew larger every day. You practiced the piano joyously, even sparked with ideas for new compositions. You were euphoric, and your doctor and all others who knew you well shook their heads incredulously over your state of well-being. But was all really well with you? Weren't you at least a bit afraid of your own courage? If not, why did you keep me a secret from your mother for so long?

Iris was in her fifth month when she finally decided to talk with her mother. At that time Katharina Sellin was sixty years old and had been a widow for twenty-nine years. Iris's parents had fled from a totalitarian country to Germany

when she was one year old. All they had brought with them from their old homeland were two suitcases and old children's songs that Iris's mother would sing tearfully to her daughter every evening. The Sellins yearned for the world they had left, and the melancholy music kept the memories of their homeland alive for years. Yet they never went back there again.

Iris's father, a physicist, died two years after they arrived in Germany. One morning he was just lying there, dead in his bed. The doctors diagnosed a cardiac infarction; Iris's mother said he died of a broken heart. Iris could not cry. She didn't understand death at age three. She grew up fatherless.

To keep herself and her daughter alive, the mother had to give up her dream of a career as a pianist. She earned their living by teaching piano, and so she gave her child what she could not have herself. And Iris, the very talented child, had practiced and learned willingly and finally achieved success.

Iris then moved to Lübeck because of the lectureship, but her mother remained in the small city in southern Germany. She was used to it there, she had friends there, her husband was buried there.

When Iris told her mother on the telephone that she was expecting a baby and was already in her twenty-second week, there was silence on the other end.

Katharina Sellin's voice sounded carefully controlled when she found words again. "Have you thought it over carefully? What about your career?"

"Don't worry about it. I have everything in hand."

"Who's the father, anyway?" her mother wanted to know.

"You'll never meet him."

"Why not?" Katharina Sellin sounded hurt.

"There is no father," said Iris. "By the way, it's going to be a girl, like me, and I'm going to call her Siri."

"What's the point of that? Iris, Siri—ridiculous. And no father? I don't understand any of this."

"We'll talk about it another time." Iris hastily said goodbye and put the receiver back in the cradle. Her hands were trembling. For the first time in her pregnancy she felt sick, terribly sick.

I know exactly why you got sick. The insight you had from this phone call must have felt like a breath of cold wind: You would be imposing your own life on me, the unborn Siri. Your daughter would grow up fatherless and driven by an ambitious mother, just like you.

Your premonition was right, Iris. All human beings repeat what has been done to them, good and bad. Even now in the clone age we are creatures of habit.

At that moment you let slip the last possible opportunity to set your clone free. But you resisted your premonition and swore to yourself at that second to do everything differently from your mother. Never would you cheat me out of a life of my own. Together we still had a chance to do it better, to avoid unnecessary mistakes that steer life onto the wrong tracks, block it, and make it difficult. You would teach your daughter everything and understand her better than anyone else. Where else was there a mother and a daughter who were also twin sisters, identical and insep-arable, actually one heart and one soul?

Why didn't you just act on your cold premonition and have me killed? Then I wouldn't be sitting here alone and without you, a half-person.

During the following weeks and months you often sat at the black concert grand and played the old children's songs for the unborn girl. The notes diffused through the wall of your abdomen, spread out in you, and enwrapped your Siri. As if you wanted to drown out all fear, that's how you played. You invoked the cycle of life, as human beings have done in their songs for thousands of years. Your hands danced wildly for Anna Perenna, the ancient Roman goddess of spring. You named your orchestral work after this goddess. It was to announce Iris's rebirth with trumpets and trombones.

C d♭ b f e, b f e d♭ c, f e c d♭ b . . .

Those are *Anna Perenna's* repeating notes. I know it so well, that round without beginning or end. It is like our two lives, like our two names: Iris-Siri-Iris-Siri. . . .

From the very beginning my development took place only in your Iris-world, in a space that was always filled with your music. The first sensory impressions my brain stored were your melodies. They were always with me as I learned, seeing, smelling, tasting. And then your famous piece *Dewdrops* came along. I bathed in its notes as the cochleas in my ears began to grow. Ever more clearly I heard and differentiated the notes, and I rocked back and forth in their rhythm. By the seventh month I was already clapping my hands and feet in time. With your music, you attuned me to the world outside, made me compliant.

And when you sometimes had doubts—you told me this later—about whether this daughter would really be all you hoped, you said to counter your fears, "Don't disappoint me, Siri! We're so much better off than other twins who have to start fighting even in their mother's body for space and food. Some even strangle each other with the cord out of jealousy. But you're growing in you, I'm carrying me in me. There's no more familiar place in the whole world."

And before you went to sleep you whispered, "Come soon, little sister. I'm waiting for you, Kehinde."

Later I learned to love this mysterious, melancholy-sounding name for the second-born twin, *Kehinde*. The name comes from the Yoruba people, in Africa, and means "one coming last." The first-born, on the other hand, is called *Taiwo*, "enjoying the first taste of the world."

Iris was Taiwo. But she did not give her twin sister the sign to follow her, as the ancients thought of first twins. Iris was already thirty years old when the cries of pain she uttered during labor called her twin into the world.

Siri Sellin was born without complications on October 12 of the year zero. Clone-baby and clone-mother were doing well. But the daughter-sister who had just slipped out of the maternal womb did not cry like other babies. Soft, barely audible sounds came from the small mouth as the midwife held the newborn high and cut the cord.

Iris claimed for the rest of her life to have recognized the first notes of the piece *Dewdrops* in the very first sounds her daughter uttered.

"She's singing my music, you hear?" she cried happily. "That's *Dewdrops*." But no one believed her.

No, I certainly did not sing when I first saw the light of the world. Probably I whimpered. At my birth, I did not announce my claim to freedom with a loud cry like all other children. Iris had already exorcised that from me.

Today I hate her music, and *Dewdrops* especially. Whenever I hear that melody I am made helpless—I feel like a fish gasping for air, just before its end.

I must bang these notes out of my head once and for all. *Bam! Bam! Bam!*

But when my forehead strikes Mr. Black's wooden body, that damned melody only cycles that much faster through the convolutions of my brain. And this cycle just will not stop: Iris-Risi-Isir-Siri-Iris-Risi-Isir-Siri.

Our names have the same sound, one sound. We were Iris-Siri and Siri-Iris. It would be a long time until the big bang, and at the beginning of our twinned existence, we actually lived in unison.

Unison
Childhood I

There wouldn't have been any me at all if it had been left up to you singletons. You would have prohibited someone like me and excluded me from your tidy family relationships. But from the beginning, my kind were cleverer than you and very determined. At first we spread ourselves as a word. We eliminated all "doubles" and instead of using the word *alike*, everyone was very modernly saying *cloned*. In this way we slowly slipped into your heads and occupied more and more thinking sites in your brains.

When you finally noticed that you could no longer get free of us, some of you tried to make us laughable, and more and more clone jokes cropped up. Others pushed us into the horror category and slaughtered us in books and films as zombies or organ providers.

But then the cloned sheep Dolly—or should I say the wolf in sheep's clothing?—came into the world showing her fangs. With this animal's first bleat, even the last human understood that we could not be stopped and were a real threat to be taken seriously. The laughing-monster screw was twisted even tighter.

Anxiety and desire spread among you. You wavered between "No, never!" and "What if...?" Prominent people were asked for their wish lists for cloning, and people continued to paint the most horrible clone scenarios. Shortly before the end of the second millennium, scientists were offering feeble reassurance: what can be done with a sheep or a mouse won't be applied to humans for a long time yet. The more intelligent among you, however, were already considering our pros and cons. And while at the beginning of the third millenium many—even if increasingly half-heartedly—were still trying to prohibit us, Iris simply acted and brought me into the world, and your worst nightmares came true.

Not even Iris could know what it would be like with us, with twice *her* and twice *I*. Even Iris was unprepared for life with her own clone.

Way before my time, cloning was compared to the first splitting of the atom, and I like that: We clones are like little atom bombs. In interpersonal relationships, we explode much of what you have held near and dear since the beginning of human thought and what appeared unalterable, yes, even eternal. After us, all that's left is a genetic Hiroshima, an emotional no-man's-land, a black desert of love.

Anyone who met Iris Sellin at the beginning of the year zero saw only a woman holding a newborn child in her arms. They could only be mother and daughter, for twin sisters are the same age and not separated by a generation. Still, deep in both of them, concealed in every individual body cell, lay the clone secret. Only Iris knew of it. But what does it mean to have the same genetic code as another if one is only a few weeks old and the other is thirty-three years old? Every person knows that there is an eternity, which can even be demonstrated mathematically. But this eternity really cannot be grasped and felt, just as cloning cannot be grasped in the beginning.

When Iris held her baby in her arms she sometimes forgot that she was rocking herself and, at the same time, her twin sister. The primeval maternal feelings swept over her then, and she lost herself in that little face. She became soft and sentimental and inhaled the soothing, sweet baby smell. She admired the little fists, held the little fingers in her hand, and enjoyed the noisy sucking at her breast. Then she was a mother like any other.

But this unfettered love did not last long. Iris was unable to surrender herself to it. This child had a purpose, and only by fulfilling this purpose did she have any meaning, did she have a right to exist. Iris could never really forget that, even if now and again she didn't think about it.

There was still no correlation of the outside world and Iris's own consciousness that she was holding her clone in her arms. And so it was almost a little helplessly that she looked at her old baby pictures in the worn, brown leather album that her mother had made for her a long time before. She compared the facial expressions in the photos with those of the little Siri she was holding in her arms. When she saw that the faces matched, a deep peace descended on her. Then she was certain that everything would turn out well.

Even you, Mother-Sister, had no more choice once I lay in your arms. Your look always contained something that exposed me and sought only you. Very deep inside me—and probably in you, too—that actually hurt terribly. But at that time, innocent, I just babbled my first sounds.

To be so different externally and still be exactly the same contradicts all human experience. That made you always be on your guard and made you so hard. For curiosity and lack of bias are needed to love a person truly and without ulterior motives.

With this clone-daughter you created a glass person for yourself: transparent from the start, explainable, free of mystery. You didn't just present me with any old life but with *your* life. Your/my genes were to develop optimally. The upbringing had to take place according to plan, carefully but consistently, and, of course, with the good intention that none of the mistakes in your own upbringing would be repeated. What a chance to survive! What audacity! But still, from the very beginning, a slightly stale feeling accompanied the triumph of having created oneself all over again.

When her daughter was three months old, Iris finally found the ideal nanny. She was named Daniela Hausmann and was almost forty, newly divorced, and a music teacher.

She was a sturdy, hardworking woman who radiated reliability. She wanted to go back to work to improve her lifestyle, because her four-and-a-half-year-old son, Janeck, was just entering kindergarten.

The work agreement that Frau Hausmann signed after some discussion expressly obligated her to develop Siri Sellin musically. She was so well suited for it that Iris took the son into the bargain, whom the nanny— she had insisted on it— might bring with her anytime.

When Janeck stood before Iris for the first time, armed with a wooden shield and a wooden sword, and cried "Your money or your life!" a deep antipathy arose between them. Hostile and bold as brass, the spindly blond boy had stared at Iris. Iris herself was surprised at how much aversion Janeck aroused in her. But then she remembered how as a child she had so wanted a big, strong brother. And what she had wanted then could not be wrong for Siri now. So why shouldn't she fulfill this wish for the child in advance? And if she wanted Daniela Hausmann, Janeck was part of the deal. Iris Sellin had no idea how vital the boy would one day be for her daughter.

Iris had more time for her practicing again, and soon her hands had remastered wide reaches and difficult crossings. She made a fair copy of the *Dewdrops* piece, for piano and clarinet, and completed the orchestral piece *Anna Perenna*, which she dedicated to her daughter. When Siri was beginning to crawl, both works were premiered in Munich.

The music critics described *Dewdrops*, which Iris herself played, as a "fine web of sounds" through which the listener was led into a beautiful park, a poetic space. But then, as with a view through a kaleidoscope, everything broke into a thousand facets. In an interview the composer explained, "I was only trying to capture life in the notes."

Iris Sellin worked hard. After all, her disease was breathing down her neck. She knew that the MS was slumbering treacherously, and so she had no pangs of conscience when she was separated from Siri. She knew about the strong twin bond that could never be broken. And as soon as Iris and Siri saw each other again, smelled and felt each other, there was a harmony and closeness between them that no singleton understands but is reported by all identical twins. Iris never had the feeling that she was missing something when she was away from Siri. Whenever she returned and took her daughter in her arms, they were very close.

These two extremes, the cool view of the clone and the deepest feelings of unity with the twin, pull on a person. They held you and me in tension for a lifetime. And so now I feel a terrible sense of disintegration, and it's tearing me in two.

Perhaps at the time I could only endure because I had my nanny—whom I called Dada — and Janeck, who liked to call me his "little sister," and whom I called Janne. I liked them both very much and loved them as my family who were always there for me. But only with you, Iris, did I feel entirely in unison.

You once explained to me what that is, unison: It is the same pitch, only an octave higher. And together we sang c^1 and c^2, eb^1 and eb^2.

I would really be lying if I claimed I was an unhappy child. The future Iris substitute thrived splendidly from the beginning, for you and I and Dada functioned perfectly. You'd considered everything in this experimental setup.

Siri learned to talk and run like any other child; she developed without abnormalities. She was hardly able to stand when she first propelled herself into her nursery to the piano with the carved legs and brass candleholders. The instrument became her favorite plaything, and as soon as she could reach the keys, she plinked around on it. When Dada played or sang for her, Siri would simply stand there and listen.

She did not go to kindergarten like Janne. Her time was filled with music lessons, taught by Iris and Dada and special music teachers from the academy. She learned all the scales and read music before she could write her letters. By age four Siri was voluntarily practicing on the piano for hours. She tried to copy every new melody she heard. She had inherited perfect pitch from her mother.

Music had by then become a necessity of life for Siri. Silence made her restless. And when she was overexcited, *Dewdrops* was the best remedy. She would lie under the black concert grand and Dada or Iris would play the piece until Siri crept out, calm again.

She spent more time with Dada and Janeck than with her mother, who was often traveling. Nevertheless, her first spoken word had been *Mama*. And when Iris was home, the little girl would sit on her lap before the black concert grand. To the right and left of her, Iris's hands conjured up the most beautiful melodies just for her. At such times, they no longer were aware where one stopped and the other began. To be so in unison was real happiness then.

You were the trunk, Iris, and I your offspring or sprout. That is exactly the meaning of the word *clone*, which comes from the Greek. All genetic descendents arising from asexual reproduction are called *clones*, such as plant cuttings or even single-celled animals that divide themselves. Later people applied the term to all artificially produced animal progeny as well. And finally humans with the same genetic information, creatures like you and me, came to be called *clones*.

Clone also means "branch." When branches are first growing and not very robust, they break easily if they are overloaded and left to their fate too early. I was still very small at that time.

You never were there when I wanted you to be. So I ask you today, dead Mother-Sister: Where were you when I was living with Janne and Dada and slowly growing bigger? They say that one time, when you'd been on tour, I even looked for you in the big grand piano.

Then after your trips, you would drop so unexpectedly and suddenly into my little child's life that it made me dizzy. You alone determined when you would appear. Your concert gowns were made of shining, stiff materials, and they rustled with your entrances. This is the sound that reminds me most strongly of our life together.

I would look up in bewilderment when you came rustling into our apartment. It was just the same later when I saw you walk onto countless stages, and each time I would be reminded of your entrances at home and become uneasy. I was the willing, grateful public, and you, Iris, were skillfully putting on an act.

Sometimes I was simply surprised that you really did exist. So my mother was not just a word, not a story, not a dream shape—she was actually standing in front of me.

One time, after a concert, you had on a long dress that was just the same blue as my very, very favorite dress. Really, I should have been nasty to you because you'd been away for so long. But that didn't happen. I could never be nasty to you, and I rushed over to you. Because we were in unison? Or was I driven by compulsion?

Anyway, Janeck always got angry that you simply had to appear and then immediately I wanted only to be with you. He felt shoved aside and was jealous of you with your "I-am-the-great-pianist airs." Janeck loved to make up expressions like that. I was an "everlastingly-around-the-piano hanger" he said, but luckily I also had my "tree-climbing brother."

Iris never stayed long, which Janeck also learned quickly. She couldn't take his little sister away from him.

She will not take you with her this time either, he said to me at Iris's funeral. I hope that's so, big Janne. But I feel so wretchedly small and desolate. And sometimes I lie down under the big piano again. I have to hide.

My hiding place lies on the island of the twins, far from

the singletons' world, into which I dare not venture again yet. I lie there with my legs drawn up and tremble. But they climb down the legs of the piano. They want to get me, the singletons. They have always hungered for us.

By year one, Mortimer G. Fisher had already published his scientific paper *Cloning* and *Parthenogenesis of Human Oocytes*. In it he had reported the first successful cloning of an adult woman by the new Fisher switching method. The publication was illustrated with the micrographs of the cell nucleus transfer, the monitor pictures of the two-, four-, and eight-celled clone, and the first ultrasonograms of the implanted fetus. The names of mother and daughter were given; Iris Sellin had agreed to it, as promised.

The paper had generated much excitement, and not only in the scientific world. All the media reported this "revolution in human reproduction" and celebrated Fisher as a "pioneer in development of the true single-parent family." Iris had posed with her little daughter in front of the concert grand for the many photographers. "Like a madonna, please!" one called out to her.

It all happened just as Iris Sellin and Mortimer G. Fisher had surmised: For some time there were excited public debates, but the cries for new ethical guidelines went unheard. An ultraconservative had also begun a laughable attempt to indict Fisher because he had violated the ethics convention still in force. But Iris Sellin was not the only one who defended Fisher. In several German and other European cities, people went into the streets and demonstrated for "full biological autonomy" and "self-determination in reproduction." To substantiate the need for cloning, Fisher himself published some typical queries he had received at his Montreal clinic, Repro.

A millionaire industrialist in his middle fifties, a bachelor, wanted to order a clone-son to later leave him his empire. The child was supposed to be born by a surrogate mother.

A singer had lost her only daughter two years before in an automobile accident. The artist's marriage could not handle this tragic event. Now the singer had turned forty and was divorced. She did not want to wait for a new life partner and future father, and she wanted a clone-daughter as fast as possible, before she entered menopause and it became too late for her to carry the baby herself.

A lesbian couple had yearned for a child of their own for a long time, but they had not been able to agree on how to go about having one. The younger woman was decidedly against using sperm from a donor. That was not only a betrayal of the lesbian idea, she said, but it might also be unhealthy for the child. For both, the clone-child—the modern immaculate conception— was a fantastic, long-sought possibility. Finally lesbian motherhood could be achieved without distasteful compromise with the male sex.

A man whose wife was incurably ill with cancer wanted to clone his wife just before her death and have the baby carried by a surrogate mother, so the dying woman might live once more through her daughter.

Parents wanted to have a clone of their fourteen-year-old son produced as quickly as possible, because he was in a coma with severe brain damage after a traffic accident and very probably would die.

A married couple asked if it would be possible to order a clone of their newborn daughter and have it frozen as a reserve embryo. From this raw material, skin or other organs could be bred for the original, if necessary.

Very soon society differentiated between the medi-clones, which, like the last case, would be bred for purely medical reasons, and the more psychologically motivated ego-clones, of which Siri Sellin was one of the first.

I of course knew nothing of all this as I groped my way through my child's world, which was so well ordered and attuned to me. But did I even have an idea—I ask myself this today—that there was a me? I mean, me as an individual person? Or can clones not even compete with the chimpanzees who pass the famous "I am I" mirror test?

Of all the creatures on earth, only humans and their ancestors, the apes, recognize themselves in a mirror, starting at about age one and one-half. If you put a colored spot on their face without their noticing and place a mirror in

front of them, monkeys as well as human children will try
to wipe the colored spot away. This is proof of the
consciousness of self, say psychologists, the beginning of the
I-feeling, the beginning of a person.

From the beginning I had only an us-consciousness, a
we-feeling. I never thought or lived without Iris, as
evidenced by the Iyou game, our first big twin secret. This
game was like my childhood: puzzling and somewhat
strange. Intimate and constricting. Serene and violating.
Full of feeling, and yet at the same time so damned calculated. Just a double game!

Iris and Siri stood very close together in front of the large
hallway mirror and held hands. At first each looked at
herself in the mirror. Iris's eyes moved over the high forehead, the unobtrusive nose, the slightly uneven left
eyebrow, the bold chin, the gray-blue eyes. At the same
time, Siri smiled into her child's face. Then they crossed
their stares and sought the eyes of the other in the mirror
reflection.

"Do you see two or four eyes?" Iris asked.

"Only two," Siri answered.

"Now you are I and I am you."

"Iyou," said the child, laughing. "YouI."

"You'll look just like me when you're big too. And then
you'll be the famous pianist," the mother said.

"I'm going to be even bigger and much more famous!"
cried Siri proudly, then suddenly asked anxiously, "Will you
already be dead then?"

"No, no!" Iris replied. "Most people get to be seventy or even eighty years old. There's a long time till then."

"Why don't people live to be three hundred years old, like turtles?"

"That's just the way it is. There's a certain life span for every different creature," Iris explained. "Our genes also control our life mechanism."

"I don't want you to die, ever! " Siri cried.

Iris hugged her and said, "Because there is you, I never will die. For I am you and you are me."

Although there is still Iyou, YouI has died. Exactly two weeks and one day ago she went away. But what can an Iyou do alone? I often stand in front of the same hallway mirror since Iris died, but I find no one. I am without consciousness of self and always was. And that was exactly the best qualification for training to be a pianist.

It was supposed to happen in me as if by itself, this love of music. "Art comes not from knowledge, but from the Muses," Iris was always saying. It's true, I had to play. Those black and white keys magically attracted me.

Or perhaps it was all different, and Iris and Dada had dragged me to the piano. Not with brutal force, of course, but with feigned love.

You trained me from the very beginning, I say now.

"I want to be a pianist, I want to be a pianist!" I repeated this sentence mechanically like a trained parrot from the time I was able to talk. And I sat at the piano like a trained monkey.

Iris would passionately deny this if she had not been silenced forever. The voice of the blood, the musical genes struck those notes, I hear her say. I inherited her talent. And then she often added, "That was I who spoke out of you. We are one, after all." Finally, she'd gotten it! From the beginning it was always only she who spoke out of me.

In the beginning was HER word.

"Why don't I have a real father, like Janne?" asked Siri when she was four years old.

That Janeck again, Iris thought with annoyance. "I didn't need a husband to have you," she answered firmly. "A doctor helped me. He took an egg out of my belly and made it come to life. And out of it came you."

"Wasn't I in your belly?"

"Yes, of course you were in my belly. The doctor put the living egg back into my belly, and there you grew just like any other child, nine beautiful months long. I called you Kehinde when I was pregnant with you."

Iris told the little girl where the mysterious name Kehinde came from. The word sounded beautiful, like music.

I always obeyed you. Not once did I tell Janeck that I was a kehinde. I kept it entirely to myself. Otherwise my big brother would have confused me with his "That can't be" and "Oh, she's making that up."

I quickly grasped that I had better keep my mouth shut, and secretly I rejoiced that I had this special mama. She was simply beautiful, and she was everything for me—mother, father, and sister, enchantress, and composer—and she loved me double, quadruple, octuple. Yes, I was very obedient and was firmly caught in the net of words you spun.

Yet even in this time of unison, there was a first sharp note of discord that disturbed our closeness. I can call up the memory of it anytime and look at it like a brilliantly clear photograph. To this very day, I remember each detail, each word spoken.

Siri was five years old when she played a piece on the piano for Oma Katharina during one of her visits.

Since Iris had told her mother exactly why Siri had no father, Katharina Sellin didn't know whether to think that was good or bad. That Iris had to be one of the first to try out this new clone method was very like her. She always wanted to be different, to outdo everyone else.

In the beginning, Katharina Sellin really only worried whether the child would be entirely healthy and normal. The growing Siri dispelled these anxieties. Still the mistrust in Katharina's look never disappeared entirely. The rare visits to her daughter grew even fewer, and she always stayed in a nearby hotel. When her grandmother traveled to Lübeck at Easter, Christmas, or a birthday, Siri avoided her eyes instinctively. The two had never liked each other.

What's the matter with me, after all? the old woman often asked herself. Why can't I simply love her like any other grandma? It was really unimportant how Siri came into the world. She was there and healthy and lively.

The child of course reminded Katharina Sellin of "her" Iris when she was a little girl. But after all, there were external resemblances in all families. And if Iris and Siri were still more alike, why get excited about it? In this way Katharina Sellin tried to reassure herself.

But when she saw Siri sitting at the piano, in the same position as Iris thirty years before, and when she heard Siri playing the same Bach fugue that had always been her daughter's favorite piece, she understood for the very first time that there were actually two of this daughter: The five-year-old Iris was playing the piano while the adult thirty-six-year-old woman was sitting by her own side.

If the two were one and the same person, then she was also the mother of both, and her dead husband was not only the father of Iris but also of Siri. The father of a child who was born after his death! These thoughts made Katharina Sellin dizzy.

Not only did the child at the piano play at least as well as Iris at the same age, she almost played better. Katharina Sellin pressed her hands against her mouth as if to stifle a scream. With effort, she got control of herself. However, Siri noticed that something unusual was happening to Oma, because suddenly she was breathing loudly and then grabbing at her mouth and throat. They looked at each other, very briefly, and Siri was frightened at how hostilely her grandmother's eyes glittered.

"Monster," Katharina Sellin hissed, then pulled herself together.

Dismayed, Iris cast a quick look toward the piano, but Siri was looking at her hands again and playing on, seemingly unconcerned.

"Did you mean me or her when you said *monster?*" Iris asked, when Siri was finally asleep and she was alone with her mother late that evening.

But the five-year-old had soon awakened from a restless sleep and clambered out of bed. When she opened the door to the hallway and heard both voices in the workroom, she had crept closer on tiptoes. Now she was standing anxiously at the door and listening, for she'd heard Iris's question about the monster very clearly.

"Both of you!" Oma Katharina's voice sounded disgusted. The girl behind the door felt her stomach lurch.

"You'll have to explain that a little more precisely," Iris demanded.

"You've taken everything from me," said Katharina. "Not only do you have a career in my place, you've destroyed my memories of the little Iris, who belonged to me alone, only to me."

"I never belonged to you!" retorted Iris.

"This damned clone has devalued everything that was important to me, my entire life, and that's all your work." Katharina's voice trembled. "I can never love Siri, and some-times I even hate you for doing this to me." Then she added, "You will bitterly regret it yet. She'll destroy you, not save you. Perhaps she'll even be the better pianist. In any case, she's even more heartless. I've seen through her. After all, I'm also her mother. Did you ever think of that, Iris?"

Fear shot through the child, who heard every word but understood nothing. How could this grandmother she had never liked suddenly be her mother?

Iris burst into a hard laugh. "My God, Mother, what's with these maledictions? You've never been easy to get along with anyhow. Since Siri came into the world, she's healed me. But you've always made me sick with your envy, your ambition, and your jealousy. I alone am Siri's mother, not you, not ever!"

"Everything you are—don't forget—you owe to me, to me alone—"

Iris interrupted her. "Please, not that again!"

"Then I'd better go," said Katharina Sellin and stood up.

Siri, confused and anxious behind the door, whisked back to her bed. She heard the front door close and the key turn twice. She pretended to be asleep when Iris came into her room and lay down beside her on the bed.

When Iris felt the child's back against her belly, she grew calm. Siri's breathing gradually became softer and more regular. She had peacefully fallen asleep. With Iris close, the sick feeling in her stomach had quickly vanished.

The next day Siri asked, "What's a monster? Why did Oma say that to me?"

"You misunderstood. She said monumental, monumentally good, because you played the Bach so beautifully and expressively," Iris answered.

Siri looked at her mother and said nothing more.

Good fairies and enchantresses never lie, Dada told me. And because I was very sure that Oma had called me a monster, you broke your own spell. Until then I'd carried an entirely beautiful picture of you within me. You were my enchantress in sounds. And when you were away, I had only to think of you and close my eyes. I'd see a movie screen, on which you appeared, looking like a vision from my fairy-tale book, wearing the blue-and-gold mantle of stars. But now you were no longer an enchantress because you'd lied to me. From that time on when I thought of you, you were just Iris.

I had to ask Janeck what a monster actually was. He screamed "AAAARGHH!" and made faces until I had to laugh. We looked at his collection of plastic horror figures and played Frankenstein and Vampire. I copied everything Janne did and practiced the monster scream until I could hardly breathe, and he laughingly admitted that I managed to do the most terrifying scream he had ever heard.

I can still do those fearful screams. Do you hear me there outside, you singletons? I am no vampire, no living-dead creature that cannot die. Don't drive a stake through my heart! begs the monster at the piano. I am only a clone, a thing who cannot live alone. When I was still small, a lying fairy cast a spell over me. Her evil curse was: You are my life. When I was six years old she bewitched me, and since then this curse has followed me.

In the spring of the seventh year, after a concert, Iris's legs failed her for the first time. She had staggered when she left the stage, then she stumbled on the steps of the theater and fell down. The next day she could no longer walk properly and, almost crippled, she was sent to the hospital. She received infusions of cortisone to control the first really severe flare of MS since Siri's birth. She was discharged after a week, on the way to improvement.

"In a few days you'll be able to walk again, though perhaps not so securely as before," her doctor told her. "You've been extremely lucky, Frau Sellin, to have had almost six years of remission."

"Has my luck run out?" asked Iris.

"That I don't know, but don't expect miracles," he advised her. "Please take it easy for a while."

At home Siri sat at the piano, her face a picture of concentration as she looked for the right notes. The child was dreadfully frightened, for her mother had been so sick that she could hardly even walk. For the first time, she had seen that even Iris was vulnerable and mortal.

Siri looked at her mother, who lay on the sofa looking unhappy. Almost grimly Siri sought a melody. She needed only to find the right one and her mother would smile again and all would be well.

She composed a little song. "That's for you," she said earnestly.

She played the piece for Iris again and again. And her mother actually smiled! She stood up—she stood there very straight—and then she came to her and laid her hands on Siri's shoulders. "I really liked that, what you just played," she said in praise.

"I'll make you well with music," the child promised.

"When you play, nothing can happen to me. That's good. You are my life."

"I am your life." Siri repeated these four words, her face serious.

I was proud when you told me, You are my life. I've been unable to forget this sentence to this day. In those days I sometimes idly smiled at myself in the mirror because I believed that I would be able to cast spells with notes just like you. In fact, we were already very similar. For you, Iris, were my life too.

The severe flare-up of her disease changed Iris Sellin. It snatched her from the false security she had lulled herself into for so long. While she lay at home recovering, she was suddenly jealous of Daniela Hausmann. She witnessed the everyday, matter-of-fact trust between her and Siri, and that reminded Iris of the times she had held her daughter in her arms and almost lost herself in that baby face. Why couldn't it be that way again? But Siri was no longer a baby, and Iris's life might end soon. She must hurry to teach her daughter everything she still had to give her. We have no more time to do anything useless, she thought as she saw Janeck run off with her daughter and didn't know where the two were going.

No one knew the secret Janeck and I had. My big brother had found out how to get into the vaulting in the roof of St. Peter's, the gothic church in the middle of the Old City island, without being seen. And when I was six years old, he took me there for the first time. Whenever there was going to be an event in the large, light nave of the church—and that happened often—a side door on the south side was left unlocked. It opened into a little anteroom in the nave. There—invisible from the church proper—was a small door to the church tower, and the caretaker left the key to it hanging above a small fuse box in the opposite corner. Quick as a wink, Janne grabbed the key, opened the tower door, and replaced the key before we slipped into the tower.

Not until we had softly closed the door behind us did Janne make any light. I pulled all my courage together and looked up the winding stairs, which twisted way up into the darkness. In single file we climbed toward the top, past the moldy-smelling, close walls. I held on tight to the greasy rope railing.

It was gloomy among the high, steep rafters, in spite of the lamps and the small roof lights. In this mysterious twilight we felt as if we were on another planet. The rounded masonry ends of the gothic arches were transformed into stone igloos, in which unknown creatures lived. Or sometimes the massive mounds looked like the backs of sleeping animals we had better not wake, refugees from an ancient time. Between the gray elevations ran a zigzag walkway made of boards. When we walked on it, the boards vibrated a little. Then Janne said, "Now we're playing Expedition."

At one place, the end stone of one of these arches could be removed. There we lay flat on our bellies and looked through the round opening down into the nave of the church. The ground lay so far down below us that it made my stomach crawl, and the people were so small I felt as though I were looking down on them from a cloud.

One day I slipped as we were hurrying down the spiral

stairs and came home with bad bruises and scrapes on my hands and face. Iris raged and wanted to know what we had been up to. Janeck shouldered all the blame, but he told her only about the church tower and the spiral staircase and was silent about the secret door and that we had been all the way up to the roof by ourselves. In a fury, Iris gave him a box on the ear and she screamed at me that never again would I be allowed to go off with that dreadful boy. What if I had broken my legs, or even my hands? That would be the end of the pianist dream! I could even have been killed!

Your illness reminded you of the reason I was in the world at all. This thought increased the pressure on you, and you increased the pressure on me. The *Iris Two* training program was to be unreeled pitilessly, and there was no place in it for an adventure-loving girl.

I probably should have told you our secret then, Iris, and you might have understood me. Janne and I possessed power over that mysterious place when we were there, up among the arches of St. Peter's. It became the best wishing spot in the world for us. We tied a string to a nail in the farthest corner and hung our rolled up wish notes on it. Sometimes we also stuck notes in cracks in the wall. On the day I fell down the spiral stairs, I had taken a piece of your music parchment, and with a golden colored pencil in my clumsy child's hand had scribbled, "I want to become a pianist." Perhaps that would have mollified you, Iris, but I didn't dare tell you that.

On the other hand, you might have had the door walled up forever. Because *you* were still the goddess. Only *your* wishes were supposed to be fulfilled, not mine.

For Siri's seventh birthday, Iris promised her a very special surprise. Someone was waiting for her in the music room, she said that morning, while the candles still burned on the birthday table. That sounded mysterious, and Siri entered the room full of expectation. But it was empty. In the center of the high-ceilinged room was only the shining black concert grand, broad and silent as always.

"There's no one here," said Siri in surprise.

Her mother took her by the hand and led her to the instrument. "May I introduce you," she said. "This is Herr Concert Grand."

"I know him already." Siri sounded disappointed.

"But from this day on you may play on him, with me and also alone." Iris saw her daughter's eyes brighten. "We three will spend much more time together now, so you must get to know him very, very well. Most musicians get to know their instruments easily, for they hold them in their hands: they blow into them, or pluck them, or beat on them. They are in very direct contact with them. With the piano it's much more difficult, so there's no musician who knows his instrument so poorly as the pianist. But it has to be different with you if you want to become a great artist."

Siri squeezed herself onto the piano stool next to Iris.

"You only love what you know," Iris explained, "and you can only play what you really love. So here, I will introduce you to one another."

Together they touched the piano's curving legs and golden pedals. They touched and named all its parts: from the keyboard cover to the music rack, from the piano lock to the hammers. Then Siri placed her ear on the top of the piano, and Iris played a chord. For the first time Siri heard something in the sounds that made her tremble with happiness.

"Crawl under the piano and thump on his belly," Iris commanded.

Enthusiastically the little girl crawled under the instrument, rolled onto her back, and struck, first with the flat of her hand, then with her fist, the wood over her.

Iris played her piece *Echoes* and made the wooden case resound. A flood of sound waves enveloped Siri and at last she exclaimed from under the piano's belly, "That's like a music shower."

Then came the keys. Siri climbed onto her mother's lap and listened to her explanations. "It's not the striking of the keys that makes the sound, but the sounding board with the hammers, which strike the strings." Together they pressed the keys covered with ivory and sought out the pressure points. They crawled almost inside the interior of the piano, made the felt-and-wood hammers move up and down, plucked the strings with their fingers, and felt the vibration of the notes.

"He ought to have a name," Siri proclaimed at the end of the hour.

"How about Mr. Black?" Iris suggested.

Siri agreed. "But we won't tell anyone he's called that," she whispered.

"It will be our twin's secret," Iris whispered back.

"Our second big secret, YouI."

"Exactly, Iyou."

From that time I submitted even more willingly to the practice program Iris developed especially for me. She knew exactly how to entice me. That I now might share Mr. Black with her actually kept me away from Janeck for a while. What more could I want since she had given me everything?

Iris Sellin was already considered one of the most successful composers of new music. At only thirty-nine years of age, she had won more than twenty international awards and prizes, received distinguished grants and countless lectureships. She still gave concerts, to be sure, but more and more often she was traveling as a composer, attending premier performances of her works or presenting her portrait concerts in talk.

After another year of unclouded twin life, Iris was asked to write an opera. She consulted her doctor, who confirmed no dramatic new changes, and then she agreed. She already had sketches and ideas in her desk drawer.

You revealed much about me/you/us in your opera, Iris. Certainly it was no accident that you chose the story of Eréndira, which was written by a South American poet in the last century.

In the story, a fat, lazy grandmother exploits her granddaughter Eréndira, who keeps house for her. The girl must work so hard that one day she falls asleep on her feet and forgets to snuff the candles. A gust of wind makes the candles flare up, and the whole house goes up in flames, along with all the miserly grandmother's possessions. The girl must sell her body to pay the damages, and the grandmother becomes a procuress who collects money from the men. She needs the girl, with whom she roams through the country, to earn money to live. But then a young man turns up who falls in love with Eréndira. She gets him to kill the grandmother. When he is arrested for murder, Eréndira flees. She only wanted justice, and in the end she became just as evil as her grandmother.

This story you set to music is an allegory of our life. Is that why the material so fascinated you?

Nine months long, every day for eight to ten hours, Iris worked on the score behind closed doors. Even when Siri drummed on the door, she didn't open it. Then Dada would hold the child tightly in her arms and comfort her. And the nanny never revealed that Janeck and Siri had again taken up their scouting trips into the city.

Janeck showed his little sister the alleys, as people called the old backyards with the small houses. From the front house, there was a low entry leading through that reminded Siri of a tunnel in a dwarves' mine. Or they went by bus to the beach, where they chased seagulls and looked in the seaweed for amber, but they never found any. Their jewels were the green glass shards abraded by the sand and sea. They gathered deserted beach chairs into a circle and made an impregnable fortress.

"What do the blood-red numbers on the wall mean,

Captain?" asked Siri.

"That's the number of my victims," whispered Janne, and he laughed gruesomely. At that Siri screeched her dreadful pirates' song, accompanied by the gulls.

They also went up in the old church vaulting again. There Siri mentioned one day how much she would like to have a cat.

"Write it down!" said Janne. "It's a good day. The sunbeams through that righthand roof light are falling exactly on the wishing string, so all wishes will be sent to heaven with the megabright speed of light."

When the opera was finally done and was going to be premiered in New York three months later, Iris wanted to take me to the opening. My emphatic "no" surprised her. She didn't know, of course, that Janeck had promised me something "so fantastic you'll die" if I would stay with him. And for the first time Kehinde did not follow Taiwo.

I chose Janne, the way children always eat the right amounts if people leave them alone. Their bodies tell them instinctively how much and what they need to grow. My soul must have felt how very much I needed Janne in order to remain healthy. I had had enough of you, Iris, and I hungered to be a normal child. Your clone was resisting becoming overstuffed with your love.

Mortimer G. Fisher received a personal invitation from Iris Sellin for the premiere of *Eréndira* at the Metropolitan

Opera House in New York, this time with only one ticket enclosed. He traveled from Montreal to see her. After the performance they quickly found one another in the middle of the drinking, chattering crowd.

"You've hardly changed," said Fisher. "I'm very happy to see you. How is your daughter?"

"Very well, thank you. I wanted to bring her with me, but unfortunately it didn't work out. She's really become very like me."

Fisher still wore a wedding ring, but they didn't speak about it this time either. Late at night, after the opening party, he accompanied Iris back to her hotel. That he would go up to her room with her was not spoken, but there was a silent understanding between them. There they stood opposite each other as they had almost nine years before when she had said to him, "Clone me!" With this sentence she had become a closely bound accomplice. Neither had forgotten this exciting feeling, nor that Iris's plea had sounded like "Sleep with me!"

The one thing they had done, the other not. And when they made love in the New York hotel, it happened with the clear knowledge that this would be the first and last time.

I am certain, Iris, that it must have been so between Fisher and you. For all people cling to the things that they know. That gives them security. And besides, to have had a child by a man you had not kissed even once was somehow laughable. The scientific archangel Gabriel consummated his union with you, the blessed virgin, but this time there

was no human being generated. On the contrary, it was
intentionally prevented.

Janeck's surprise for Siri was a small black cat with one
white paw. "That's a black piano with a single white key,"
he joked. "And when you press on it, it mews."

Siri flung her arms around Janeck then stroked the little
animal that was now going to belong to her alone. Iris had
always refused to buy a pet because supposedly it would
distract her too much.

Siri carried her little darling throughout the entire
apartment, even taking her into the music room, where she
struck some notes on the piano for her. The cat perked up
her ears. In Iris's workroom, Siri let her attention wander
for a moment. The cat hopped out of her arms and landed
on the long wood table where the papers on which Iris
wrote her music were still lying. Frightened by the rustling
parchment, the kitten sprang wildly around. The large
sheets of paper slid down, and the bottle of ink, which
hadn't been tightly closed, fell over and emptied over Iris's
work. Some of the sheets were spattered with black.

Siri caught the cat and soothed her with tender words,
but she was trembling with fear. Iris should not have gone
away, she thought. This serves her right. I'll simply throw
the pages away and not say that it was you, my kitten.
Otherwise you won't be able to stay.

She named the cat Isabella and whispered softly in her
ear: "Now you are my life."

You were standing in the door again, back from America. But this time I didn't run to you, and I held my cat fast in my arms. You looked at me angrily when you saw my dirty hands and the scratches Isabella had made. I also had on my most colorful frilly dress because I knew you didn't like it.

When I'm afraid or have stage fright, my left eyebrow twitches, just like yours. This twitching placated you, because you found yourself in me again. And then for the first time you came to *me* and took me and the cat into your arms.

"Siri, you are my life," you whispered. And when I heard your voice, my fear vanished. You smelled so good, of deepest closeness. Your smell and your voice always went through and through me. I had to just put my arms around you, listen to you, nuzzle the curve of your neck, and immediately I loved you infinitely and forgave you everything. I forgot the tears I'd shed when you were away and forgot my rage at your work that stole our time together.

That is how you always got me, twin sister. With this embrace you rendered me helpless. And if you had asked me at that moment to give my cat away and never see Janeck again, I would have promised you that. A short time later, I voluntarily gave Isabella to a girl in the neighborhood. For after the special concert in Hamburg, I no longer wanted a cat that could distract me.

One of the first fall storms swept over the Autobahn on that September evening as we were driving toward Hamburg. I sat with Janne and his mother in the first row of the concert hall and really everything was the same as always. Yet suddenly I felt as if I were hearing your music for the first time. You had prepared me for this concert more than usual. At the end, when everyone was clapping, you came down from the stage, took me by the hand, and pulled me up to the footlights. There we bowed together.

"Soon we'll be appearing together," you whispered to me onstage. I was the only one who heard amid the loud applause of the audience.

When I rode back to Lübeck with Dada and Janne, I crawled into the backseat to be far away from them. They should not be able to push in between you and me. Suddenly I felt like a stranger between the two of them. In everything I did from that point on, I had one goal only: to appear with you.

Something had changed during the concert. Today I know what: At that time I began to be aware of me/you/us. And during the entire ride, Iris, I heard you whispering, "You are my life, you must practice! Practice more!" So I gave away my cat.

That evening, as the raindrops pattered against my window, I cried myself to sleep. My childish fear was mixed with the frightening and delicious anticipation of finally playing duets with you.

Duet
Childhood II

Suddenly the name was there, just like that: Motwi. It sounded quite funny. When I said both syllables short and high, it almost sounded like birds twittering, and when I said "Motwi" gently and drawn out, it was a beautiful pet name. But I could also say "Motwi" sharp and cuttingly. Then I bellowed the *Mo* like a command, very short and hard, so that the *twi* then had to trail along, like a little peep.

Motwi means mother-twin, and the name occurred to me just before my eighth birthday. Before that time I had only mechanically repeated everything I heard. Now I was thinking independently and began slowly to understand, and to feel, what it meant to be not only a twin but a clone-twin. Perhaps that's why I invented this name for you, Motwi.

In the second grade everyone had to construct their family tree on the computer. Siri left the space for "Father" blank, and the teacher corrected her: "That won't work, Siri. Everyone has a father. At least you can put in 'unknown' or 'parents divorced'."

"But I'm cloned. My mother didn't need a man to have a child." To Siri this was entirely normal, and she was annoyed at the other children who began to giggle. "I don't have parents. I have only *one* clone-parent, and that's my mother."

"Clone-parent—but I've never heard of that," said the teacher.

"That word is my own invention," replied Siri proudly. The boys and girls burst out laughing and started whispering to one another.

"Quiet now!" the teacher commanded. "And, Siri, you can leave that space empty. We'll see whether our geneaology program will accept it or report an error." Again some children laughed. Siri wondered what was so funny about it.

That evening she told her mother about the incident, and Iris reassured her. There had been cloned children for a number of years now, yet some people still thought these children are genetically manipulated people. Stupidity would never be eradicated.

And Siri asked Iris, "Do I really not have a father? Please explain it to me one more time."

From her writing desk, Iris produced the carefully saved article by Mortimer G. Fisher about his first human cloning. She showed Siri the photographs and explained how an Iris-clone was made of one Iris egg cell, and that they were exactly like identical twins.

"And they understand each other, so they like each other especially well," said Iris. Together they admired the picture of the two-celled Siri-Iris and then the picture of the Siri-Iris fetus. "There you were just sixteen weeks old."

"Then you're my motwi," cried Siri, clapping her hands.

"I beg your pardon?"

"My mother-twin! Motwi, motwi," Siri trilled.

"I could get used to that. It sounds like a lot of fun."

"And then a boy-clone has a fatwi! Fatwi!" Siri repeated her invented words, delighting in her marvelous idea.

We drew closer and closer together in those years. All individuality was successfully driven out of me. I was you with all my heart and in everything I did. My look as a child was astonished and sometimes bewildered. I was addicted to you, Motwi. Other parents called our relationship close. Yet I still wanted to be somewhere else. Where, I didn't know, but perhaps my excursions with Janne into the city or to the church vaulting were the expression of this slowly growing longing.

Sometimes I was uneasy in ways I couldn't explain, but I didn't yet grasp the rules of Clonopoly. I did what you told me to. Please draw a card! It says: I want to become a great pianist.

I practiced willingly and diligently—hours long, days long, months long—and the muscles that moved my heavy little fingers became very strong. This was significant, for the littlest finger, the one everyone always underestimates, is the most important player. It strikes the highest and the deepest notes. The little fingers on each hand hold everything in between them together. But what held me/you/us together?

Siri had no problems in school. She mastered the subjects almost without trying. Her schoolmates knew that she wanted to be a pianist and that her mother was a famous composer. They understood too that she had little time for play. Siri was quiet and disturbed no one, and so the children accepted the aura of specialness that surrounded her from the beginning. She was not arrogant, but there was always great distance between her and the others in her class. Sometimes other mothers and fathers looked enviously at the almost palpable harmony in the Sellin family, and they would secretly wish that their sons and daughters were less rebellious and were as loving as Siri was to her mother.

Uniovular, or identical, twins are not really from one egg alone. We soon learned that in school. "They owe their life to an egg and a sperm cell that are united," our teacher explained after I'd announced that I was a clone. "On the other hand, in the fraternal, or binovular, twins, two eggs are fertilized at the same time and grow along together. In identical twins, the egg cell splits into two parts after it has been fertilized."

Now, of course, I know that scientists speak only of "monozygotic" twins when they mean identical twins, and we clones—correctly speaking—are artificially produced monozygotic twins.

At a certain point, if separated, the cells of an embryo lose their capacity to develop into twins. Many researchers equate this moment with the beginning of individuality.

And so it's only a logical conclusion that the production of a clone, like me, requires regression to a zygotic state, in which all individuality is exorcized.

The apartment in Lübeck was a place separated from the normal world. Mother's and daughter's attachment surrounded their home like a high fence. Siri closed out her school friends, and Iris kept out men. Her travels offered enough opportunities for brief affairs, and if she met with a man more often, Iris made sure that he arrived after Siri was asleep and left before morning.

It had been some time since Thomas Weber had been the first to hear Iris's new compositions, now that she played her music for her daughter first. It wounded her old friend to have lost this privilege, and he found it simply ludicrous as well. To let a schoolchild issue judgments on new music!

"Why?" Iris asked him. "She has an elemental feeling for music, especially my music. Children are much keener than adults and not so cerebral. They don't carry around the entire history of music the way we do, so they don't need to classify things."

Iris grew more and more dissatisfied with her own piano playing, however. The multiple sclerosis was slowly making impossible the small movements that brought her music to life. Her shoulders, arms, hands, her joints, her entire body could no longer convey what she felt. All the nuances were lost. On the very worst days she was glad just to strike the right keys. On such evenings Iris sat beside

Siri's bed and looked at the sleeping child, her clone. Iris watched her until she was reassured by the ever more apparent similarities.

Did you go through the scientists' lists and check off me/you/us? After all, monozygotic twins are required to share some external characteristics: color, quality, and thickness of hair; hair patterns on the face, neck, and hands; length, thickness, shape, color of, and distance between eyebrows; color and structure of the iris of the eye; width, shape, and angle of the eyelids; the various cranial measurements; length, width, and shape of the nose; shape and placement of the teeth; shape and position of the ears; chin shape; body height; skin color and special skin characteristics such as freckles; blood supply; shape of the hands and fingers; and fingerprints. What's more, identical twins have identical brain waves.

And so you could see into me as into a mirror, and you knew exactly what was going on inside me. Otherwise, how would you have managed so easily to talk me out of the violin? The elegant style of the instrument had once fascinated you and then your daughter. So you pulled your father's old violin out of the cupboard and made the strings screech horribly. That's what your mother had done when you were young, too.

"A piano can never sound so wrong," you said. "A piano is a music machine that creates notes by itself. You must only let them sound."

I held my ears and cried, "Horrible!" and "Eeeek!" Then

I sat down contentedly at the piano again.

For me the normal world hardly counted at all, only the Iris world. I suffered even more, then, when you immersed yourself in your world of notes and were unreachable to me. Because of the illness, you had to use the time when you were feeling well. But I looked away when you were feeling bad and when your hands trembled. Small children are afraid of illness.

I wanted a healthy mother. And so I had to play even better, to help you, just as had happened when I was six years old and you couldn't walk anymore. You praised me then, saying "You are my life." Yes, I am your life, Motwi.

Siri no longer drummed on the workroom door or screamed and wept for Iris when she had no time for her. Only a bitter expression distorted her small mouth. And when Dada asked her what was wrong, Siri became sulky. Either she said nothing or—and this happened more and more often—she reviled her nanny and accused her of always siding with Iris.

When Siri felt cast out of the close twosome, she went into the music room. She darted across the parquet floor on tiptoe, so as to not disturb Iris in the adjoining room, and she lay down under Mr. Black's wooden belly. There she was reminded of the solemn mood in a church, of a spell that could be broken by too-noisy footsteps. But the nine-year-old girl no longer believed in the enchantress and her spellbinding music. She now knew that such things only happened in fairy tales.

The word clone never appeared in any of my fairy tale books, because they were too old-fashioned. However, many twins romped through the stories—Jorinda and Joringel, and in another book, Lisa and Lottie. I could spell, write, and read clone but not grasp it. Sometimes, when you hear a name from a foreign country, the sound awakens a desire to travel there and actually see and experience the village, mountain, or river. Cloneness was for me, as a child, like a village in a foreign country where I had never yet *really* been.

On my ninth birthday, Iris and I planted a small gingko tree in our garden. She told me that its almost heart-shaped leaves were an ancient twin symbol and therefore brought health and happiness, and I blindly believed her.

At the end of the ninth year, a second clone outing made headlines, and it was occasioned by the founding of the Commission for Reproductive Progress (CPR). Reproductive cloning had already become established, and from that point on it was to be governmentally controlled.

"We live in a post-Hippocratic age. For a long time it has not been the physician who has had the last word, but the patients," stated cloning pioneer Mortimer G. Fisher in an interview. Professor Fisher and his colleagues had been encouraging clone parents and their offspring, or clonoids, to publicly acknowledge their manner of reproduction. Newspapers and magazines seized the topic anew, and the question "Cloned children, yes or no?" was again the theme of countless talk shows.

That a clone child would be deprived of one parent could not be an argument against cloning. Already more and more children were living with so-called single parents. The clone child merely experienced the single-parent family consistently, from the very beginning.

Psychologists also dismissed the objection that the clone child could not develop its own identity. Precise studies of identical twins had shown that this would very probably be the case. But this finding was also reassuring, for it exposed as irrational the fear many people had of human clones. If a cloned child is simply a direct copy, a blueprint as it were, of an entirely normal person, the child too is therefore completely normal.

Mortimer G. Fisher did not believe in the myth of split souls either. It lacked any biological foundations, he thought. Yet, all plants, animals, and even humans are—in a certain sense—slaves to their genes. No one of them can change its spots, not even the supposed crown of creation, *Homo sapiens*. The clone would, like all normally conceived creatures, be released into a fierce battle between heredity and environment. There she would fight for survival, to show what she had and what she made of it. Everyone makes her own way, whether a clone or nonclone.

Besides, nature itself does this experiment: In every one thousand births, there are reliably three to four pairs of identical twins, who are, after all, natural clones. Why should artificial twins be particularly unnatural? Clones separated by a generation might perhaps be freer than ordinary identical twins, who must share not only their genes but also their life span.

"One thing a clone will never be is a mindless body shell," intoned Fisher in a discussion roundtable. "It's no longer a matter of prohibition. Clones have been living among us for years. But we still battle against prejudice. Clones are human beings like you and me, and we should let them live."

Iris let me live, but only on our island. And so I dreadfully missed Janeck, my "tree-climbing brother." I thought wistfully of the scouting trips with him and the forbidden hours in the church vaulting, which had become rarer and rarer until they had stopped altogether. It was partly because at this time, when I was not quite ten and Janne close to fifteen, there was an awkwardness between us. I was still a child, while he already had stubble on his chin. Other boys had teased him for running around with the little Sellin kid all the time. And then when Janne fell in love for the first time, I was angry and jealous of this Karin, whom I didn't even know. When Janeck then called me to say he was sorry he couldn't come to my birthday dinner, I screamed into the receiver that I never wanted to see him again. And once again Iris consoled me by promising me a very special birthday surprise.

The present from Iris was a 450-page score. "Dedicated to my Siri on her tenth birthday" was written on it. Siri read the title, *The 35th of May*, and beamed. Her mother had composed an opera for her from one of her favorite books. The book by Erich Kästner, with the beautiful subtitle, "Conrad's Ride to the South Seas," was a book Iris had also loved as a child.

Several days later mother and daughter watched the rehearsals for this opera, which was to have its premiere in a few weeks. And for a short time Siri forgot Janneck completely, captivated as she was by Uncle Ringelhut, his nephew Conrad, and the horse Negro Caballo, who walked through a closet to enter strange worlds.

I always loved the third scene of the opera best, in which Ringelhut and Conrad land in the "turned-around world." Only children could enter this world, and children decided everything. They were the rulers, while teachers and parents sat on school benches.

Perhaps I liked this world best because it was the extreme opposite of my own: Iris decided everything about me—not just like other parents, but in the most fundamental ways you can think of. She had made me into herself: "You are my life, don't ever forget that!"

The doctor to whom I owed my life traveled to the premiere of *The 35th of May*. Mortimer G. Fisher came to our house the afternoon before opening night. I was incredibly eager to see him, but when he at last stood before me I was strangely unmoved. I thought he was pleasant, that he looked nice with his round glasses, but otherwise I felt nothing. Perhaps I had expected too great a feeling for him and so was let down.

But then I saw his beautiful hands with the long, narrow, elegant fingers. Even though Iris had explained to me hundreds of times that there were no special pianist's hands, that my skill depended only on technique and speed of reaction, and on the "inner hearing" in my head, I still hated my sturdy Sellin hands with their short fingers.

If Fisher had been my real father, I might have inherited his hands. When this thought shot through my head, I was no longer indifferent to the man. I was angry at him because he had not become my father. And I was angry at Iris because she had not wanted me to have such beautiful hands.

That night I wept for the father I would never have and for whom I longed so terribly. Perhaps the man with the beautiful hands *was* my father, and Iris had kept it to herself because he was married? For a long time after that, I persuaded myself that I was the illegitimate daughter of Mortimer Gabriel Fisher.

On Mother's Day of the twelfth year, Thomas Weber organized a concert in which Iris and Siri Sellin were to share the second half.

There was no great risk in such a Mother's Day concert. The public was receptive, since it was not only a mother and daughter but the Sellin twins who were appearing. The advance ticket sales went well, and eventually there were even inquiries about buying the television rights to the second part.

Iris had included *Dewdrops* in the program. As in earlier performances, she was going to tell something beforehand about when it originated—that is, during her pregnancy with her clone, Siri.

Siri had refused to put on the boring black dress her mother had picked out for her. "We're not going to a funeral. It's Mother's Day!" It didn't matter to Siri that a black dress was the usual costume for such an event. "Then today we're going to be unusual," she said.

Finally Iris threatened to cancel the concert if Siri didn't put on the dress.

Siri had no choice. Ten minutes before her entrance she went to the ladies' room, where she pulled out a four-inch-wide, stridently yellow taffeta ribbon that she had stuck inside her tights as a flat roll. She wound it several times around her hips and made a magnificent bow. When she stood next to Iris again, the mother took no notice at all of the daughter's change, and Siri was so angry that all her stage fright was simply blown away.

The introduction by the announcer was underway when Iris took her daughter by the hand and Siri forgot all her resentment. Beaming, the two walked out onto the stage where the grand piano sat in the spotlight and the television cameras awaited them.

That ridiculous entrance on Mother's Day! And you didn't even see my yellow sash. I only wore it because I wanted you to see *me* finally. Before the concert you simply disregarded me. You showed me around as you: my clone, look! Isn't it amusing? All that was left to me as protest were colorful clothes and flashy ribbons. What else can an eleven-year-old do? If you'd been angry about it, I would have known: I am someone. But you didn't even allow me that little triumph that day. You deliberately ignored the yellow ribbon!

Janeck had come to the Mother's Day concert; his mother had asked him to. When the two came backstage with a gaily colored bouquet for Siri, Janeck whistled approvingly through his teeth. "Little Sister, what's happened to you? You're a real oh-please-kiss-me woman." And he very boldly planted a kiss on her mouth.

Siri didn't know what to do with her hands or where to look. "Don't," she said. "Big brothers don't do things like that."

"I forgot that," said Janeck, poking her in the side. Softly he said to Siri, "Will you come with me to the vaulting? We'll hang up some new wishes." Siri shook her head, but she smiled at the same time. Janne wouldn't give up, so they whisperingly made a date for the next afternoon. Iris, who was now approaching them, mustn't notice anything.

The next day Siri lay on her stomach as she used to and looked through the round opening.

This gaze into the depths below gave me a tingly feeling like the one I'd more recently been feeling when I saw Kristian, one of Iris's friends.

Probably he wasn't in the apartment any more often than other men before him. But I'd never been interested in them, and so I'd never taken any notice. The first thing that made me aware of Kristian was his voice. Hearing it one night, I liked it so much that I decided to get to know this man. I kept trying to stay awake, waiting for that voice. And one evening it was actually there again, in the kitchen. Excitedly I'd gotten up and gone to the kitchen, and Iris had to introduce me to Kristian. I'd had bad dreams, I said, and got myself a glass of water.

Kristian's voice was even more wonderful close up, like a Mahler symphony. He was an architect here in Lübeck, but he traveled often, and he was ten years younger than Iris, twenty years older than me. When I said good night to both of them and Kristian smiled at me with his brown eyes, I had this funny feeling for the first time.

Iris noticed that Siri often came in when she was sitting with Kristian. This disturbed her, but she didn't say anything. It probably has to do with a father fantasy, she explained to her friend, who nodded understandingly. "It'll pass," he said.

"Do you really like her, my daughter? I mean, do you like her very much?" Iris asked.

"How could I not like her when she looks almost exactly like you!" replied Kristian. "But she's so young. I like mature women much better."

Iris's laugh annoyed the child, who had again slipped out of bed and was listening at the door.

In spite of that, we approached the summit of harmony. We were a perfectly coordinated duo, hardly able to become any closer. But there in the high peaks the air gets very thin: twin-love, we learned, can take one's breath away.

The Iyou-YouI game slowly turned serious. We looked more and more alike with every day, with every week, and soon we would no longer need to pretend to be twins.

I was twelve years old when I got my first period. I drank a glass of champagne with Iris and we clinked glasses because I was a woman.

"You are still my life," Iris said. And for the first time I did not answer her, but silently asked myself, But my life, where is my life?

I did not have father fantasies. I asked myself why Kristian was not really in love with me, the younger edition of Iris.

One morning, when I was thirteen, I wanted to look at myself in the bathroom mirror but saw only my mother. Why was I so frightened? After all, I knew that I was her twin—almost the same size now, similarly talented, the same in appearance. Why was I so terribly frightened?

I winked at the one in the mirror, but she wouldn't turn back into the girl I'd been the day before. Only when I cried at her, "Good morning, Siri! Brush your teeth!" was I back to myself again. And I swore never again to put on one of Iris's nighties. But it wasn't the nightie's fault. My soul was sick of Iris, and of looking for Siri.

To the singleton world, they were still a picture of harmony. They appeared to be living their dreams. Siri gave small concerts more and more often and played her mother's compositions. The condition of Iris's health fluctuated, but there was no dramatic deterioration.

Then in the spring of the fourteenth year, a sudden, loud discord destroyed the twin-harmony. One day as Siri was sitting at the piano, on the stool with the blue cushion playing *Echoes*, without warning she toppled forward like a doll. The dull thump on the keys was followed by a hideous chord. Iris screamed and pulled her daughter up, embraced her upper body with both arms and pressed her to her. She rocked Siri back and forth like a little child, stroked her face, and implored, "Please wake up, my little one!" Siri wished that this rocking might never end.

"She's had a brief faint, just a circulatory insufficiency," the doctor said. "That can happen at this age when all the hormones are changing."

He was right, Iris thought. Puberty was surely to blame, and the fact that Siri had been practicing too much recently. But that dissonant chord had disturbed her.

At that time it was always just "we." For years it was only *we*. As a child I had not learned to say *I*. I loved you too, very much. Only this *We* existed, all-powerful and over-powering. I was stuck in the straightjacket of this twin-love. It immobilized me, it tied my hands firmly to my body. And so playing cost me more and more strength.

As an immature, clumsy adolescent girl, still somewhat chubby, with too-long arms, I asked myself: How will I ever become like you? In my eyes, you were just as beautiful and successful as ever. And I wanted to be that way too—but suddenly I also didn't. I practiced like mad to please you and was afraid of your criticism. I hated those exercises, yet I only wanted to practice, practice.

To sow conflicting feelings in a person is to divide them in two. I cried for help, but there was no one, no father who might have protected and reassured his little daughter.

My body, which more and more resembled yours, was the first to rebel against this gigantic We, long before my brain understood. My brain didn't want to understand. After all, our brain is a twin-thing with its two Siamese halves. And everybody knows twins stick by each other.

I'd blindly followed you into this hall of mirrors, lured by magic words and deceived by distorted images. You alone savored the world. You had fed yourself full and round on your success and then on me too. I trotted after you like a simpleton, year after year. Then one day I was no longer a child, but I was still not a real woman either.

The We was suddenly more gigantic than it had ever been, and it frightened me. How should I find myself when in my search I only bumped up against you, against your image and your image of me? Whatever I did, you were there before me. You had done everything first and better. I was only supposed to be your life, all over again.

You always forgot the child. It was only when I hit my head on the keys that you looked at me and became the mother who comforted me and simply took me in your arms, without any ulterior motive. I kept my eyes closed longer than necessary, not wanting that holding I had missed so ever to end.

Now, Iris, you can never hold me again or comfort me, even if you wanted to.

Siri slipped completely into her mother's skin for the first time when she was fourteen years old. Carefully she drew a fine line on her eyelids, put on mascara, and picked out one of Iris's lipsticks. No one would notice the one-and-one-half-inch difference in size between her and her mother if she wore high heels and put on her mother's gray twin set.

In front of the mirror, using the same gestures as her twin, she brushed her hair behind her ear and commanded, "Iris, go to the hospital! Oma Katharina is waiting for you."

The old woman had fallen ill with a bad flu during a visit to Lübeck, and it had affected her circulation. It was a matter for concern in a woman over seventy, her doctor had said, but Iris had left the country anyway and gone to the United States. She couldn't possibly cancel the week-long composition workshop that had been planned for so long and that was, as usual, fully booked. She'd begged her daughter to visit her grandmother at least once or twice while she was away.

"Okay, I'll represent you."

Iris had not picked up on the double meaning of the words.

Siri regarded the other one in the mirror with satisfaction. All identical twins play such comedies of errors, and she finally was able to enjoy this pleasure too.

She didn't have to practice Iris's walk, her gestures, or her laugh—that all came on its own. Siri knew that sometimes her voice wasn't the same. But she knew well how Iris's voice changed when she spoke with her mother. A slightly aggressive undertone accompanied every word, like a second melody. Siri practiced the line, "Hello, Mama, how are you?" until she thought she could imitate the perfect Iris voice. Her grandmother could see almost nothing anymore, so she heard that much better.

At three in the afternoon, the false Iris entered the sickroom. "Hello, Mama, how are you?" The nurse, who was fluffing the pillows, only glanced at her and then left the room.

The patient was surprised. "I thought you were in America," she said.

"I canceled the trip because of you," Siri answered, and Oma Katharina looked at her in astonishment. For a moment Siri was afraid her exaggeratedly friendly tone had betrayed her.

Touched and speechless, Katharina Sellin reached for Siri's hand and stroked it with her fingers. Siri withdrew from the grasp before her grandmother could sense the deception by touch.

Iris's double turned up at the hospital on the following two days and duped the old lady again. This Iris agreed with her mother about many things at last. Yes, yes, it was true, she had only her to thank for her career. And about that daughter—better not to say anything about her.

When Siri left the hospital after the third visit, the ward doctor ran after her with a CD in his hand.

"Excuse me, Frau Sellin," he cried. "I missed you upstairs on the floor. Would you please give me your autograph?

With tomorrow's date? It's my wife's birthday."

"But . . . " Siri quickly dropped her head.

The doctor did a double take, looked at the photo on the CD cover and then at the woman who stood before him. "Oh, my goodness! You're the daughter. I actually mixed you up with your mother," he apologized.

"I can sign it for you anyway," Siri said with a smile. "One Sellin is just like the other, and our signatures are quite similar."

Somewhat hesitant and embarrassed, the doctor handed her his pen and Siri wrote Iris's name right across the photo.

In the days that followed, Siri did not go to the hospital as promised and did not telephone. When Iris returned from America a week later and visited her sick mother, the old lady immediately reproached her: "What's the matter with you? Why are you treating me like this? First you come every day and then you don't visit me at all anymore, and you don't even bother to pick up the phone."

"But I was—" Iris swallowed the rest of the sentence. It was immediately clear to her that Siri must have pulled this trick.

For the first time Siri had taken her place and totally substituted for her, and Iris could even take pleasure in that. She smiled at her mother and said, "I simply had too much to do."

I never again lost that practiced voice with which I had deceived Oma Katharina. From then on that aggressive undertone accompanied my every word to you, Motwi, like a low melody. Just one more similarity—a bitter lesson for dumb little Siri, who really only wanted to be different. Whatever I did, I became more and more like you. I could not change my/your/our spots!

When Oma Katharina died a few weeks later of an embolism, I refused to go to her funeral. For I had never really forgiven her for the "monster" comment, although today I have to admit she was right: We/you/I became monsters, twin-monsters.

You didn't scold me after the hospital act, but a scolding was exactly what I wanted. I hadn't wanted to annoy Oma Katharina but to provoke you. But you only laughed and asked, "Why didn't you discuss it with me? Working together makes a trick like that much more fun. Who shall we fool next?"

"How about Kristian?" I asked. Your face turned stony. Finally, with a troubled smile, you replied that that would not be an especially good idea. And after that you looked at me differently from before. For the first time you saw me as a rival—you saw me alone. Now I knew how I could get to you.

Kristian was no longer able to sit lightheartedly across from Iris and Siri. When one day he unconsciously compared the appearance of the two and Siri pleased him more, he was deeply shocked and ashamed of himself. His and Siri's eyes had met only briefly, but he was certain she had seen into him.

After that he smiled at her more rarely, and Iris asked him, "Why are you suddenly so cool to Siri?"

"She gets on my nerves. She's really become too old for

me to be worshiped as a father substitute."

Iris said, "I'll talk with her—"

But Kristian interrupted her harshly, "Please leave it alone. Let me take care of it my own way. I'll just come here less often and instead we'll meet at my place."

Iris nodded, but she was uneasy about it.

The Iyou-Youl game had to have consequences. And one consequence of the twin-act was that I actually fell in love with the same man as you. The rules of Clonopoly, Iris, are even-handedly merciless! But suddenly you didn't want to play anymore, you spoilsport.

The next time I climbed up into the vault with Janne, there was a special wish note in my pocket. "I am in love. I want him to love me too," it said. I'd left out the name so that I could show my wish to Janeck, as we'd arranged.

"So who's the lucky one?" he asked. "Is it me?"

"Don't be so conceited," I said.

"What isn't true now can still happen," he said with a laugh.

"But then I wouldn't have a brother anymore." My voice sounded so serious and I must have looked so scared that Janeck put his arm around me and promised very solemnly never to fall in love with me.

During those years when Siri was changing from child to woman, Iris was constantly amazed: Her plan had actually been realized. There was her beautiful, healthy daughter who was well on her way to becoming an outstanding pianist. The piano lessons at Mr. Black still united the two twins. Their need to express themselves in music and that obsession to feel the notes together still blocked out discord. When they played duets, Iris felt through and through that everything was right. She could love her daughter and her youth. She could feel young again. She felt like a goddess, enthroned high over all, and seemed immortal.

But more and more often, Iris experienced dark moments. The multiple sclerosis granted her no more remissions. Beginning in the fourteenth year, the flares became more frequent and more severe. On some days they turned Iris into an old woman, who even wet her bed now and again. She was just in her mid-forties, but at such times she moved like an ancient.

Anyone looking in an ordinary mirror sees whatever she wants to. She becomes young again with a little smile, and with a turn of her head she changes into the young woman she wants to be.

Siri's face left Iris no room for such illusions, and that was what made this living mirror so unbearable. The second Iris was no longer a consolation, and increasingly often she became a torment. It was especially painful for Iris to constantly see her as a blooming woman when she herself felt so bad. Jealousy and envy made her bitter and more severe with her daughter.

She observed Kristian sharply and thought she discerned a special lighting of his eyes whenever he encountered Siri. And really, why shouldn't Siri attract him? She was just like Iris, after all, only she was obviously younger and, ever more often, more beautiful. Jealousy poisoned Iris's thoughts.

My feelings also became increasingly conflicted. The more I resembled you, the stranger I felt in my own body, which I regarded mistrustfully. It did not belong to me but to you. I no longer wanted to be like you, but as a clone I had no choice, and I developed according to my/your/our genetic code.

That twins are in an eternal battle with one another is ancient human knowledge. They embody light and darkness; they are symbols for good and evil. They are revered in many religions as something special. And because twins can bring harm as well as good, they have to be placated so they only employ their positive powers.

I'd long ceased to be a child and someone easily kept in a good mood. Now there were two women living on the twin-island, and it was too small. My colorful clothes were like war paint, and there could no longer be peace.

Your Lifeline was taking a downward turn, Iris, and mine was still rising. Where they crossed, it had to come to a duel. I or you, you or I? We split apart on the threshold of adulthood. The time had come when I finally comprehended it all, and discord had to begin.

Discord
Youth I

I feel blue means I'm sad. Blue can also describe bad language. Blue always has two faces. Blue is the cold laboratory light in which our relationship began. And blue can be as beautiful or corny as the most gorgeous summer sky or the Blue Grotto of Capri. Being a *blueprint* also has two sides: there's twin lovey-doveyness and cold calculation; the greatest love and the deepest hate.

The slaves sang the blues because they longed for freedom. And I had the blues too. I'd never been a true twin, only her clone. I realized this at fifteen, when I went to a twins' convention without Iris.

Siri had told her mother that she was spending a seaside weekend with Janeck again. Her big brother, who was soon going to be studying law in Hamburg, had just bought a beat-up old station wagon and Siri didn't have to beg to get him to drive her to Dibbern.

"Why are you so keen to go to this—what was the

slogan?" he asked as they were underway.

"Alike as two eggs . . . something like that."

"That's so bad it hurts!" said Janne with a laugh.

"You don't have to come with me, you know. I just want to find out what it's like."

"What what's like?" Janeck asked.

Siri shrugged her shoulders and didn't answer.

After they'd found a cheap room in Dibbern in a little pension, Janeck drove her to the city hall at the edge of town. Over the entrance hung a banner saying, "First International Twins' Convention" in large letters. There were pots of flowers on each side of the open glass door. Siri turned and waved to Janeck before she disappeared into the building.

When Siri registered, the secretary checked over her registration form and asked whether her twin sister would be coming later.

"Unfortunately she's ill with a bad case of the flu," Siri lied.

"Too bad. Then you can't take part in our main contest tomorrow. We're looking for the couple that look most alike—and you're identical twins?" the secretary asked.

"More than identical," said Siri. "We're one egg copied, really cloney. Nothing random about us!"

"You have a good sense of humor," said the secretary. "Maybe the other contest would be something for you. We're going to look for the best twin jokes tomorrow."

The mayor was just beginning his welcoming address when Siri entered the bright auditorium. She tried to work her way to the front, but the people in the audience were standing too close together. "Duos, and twins in particular, are the trend," declared the man on the podium. "They express the spirit of the times. Our modern society—with the Internet and its worlds of images, its single-child families and singles—has become the loneliest of all worlds. More and more often, we all seek stronger security and community. The I-times are coming to an end, and the we-generation is on the advance—so claim the sociologists and cultural critics. And you, by gathering here today, are very special representatives of this new we-feeling. A cordial welcome to all twins and their parents!"

The mayor looked into the broadly smiling faces, most of which were doubled and in a few instances tripled. Among the drinking and applauding pairs, the single distressed face of a fifteen-year-old nobody was conspicuous. Siri felt lonely in this world, and she realized that twins planned such meetings to be the rule rather than the exception.

After the scheduled "informal get-together," the countless pairs of twins, ranging in age from two to seventy-five, gathered on the auditorium stage for a group photograph. Unfortunately she could not be in the picture, Siri told one of the organizers who was trying to get her onstage. Her twin sister was seriously ill.

Then there were magic shows, and many twin parents traded twin clothes and twin baby carriages. Siri watched for a long time as a portrait artist captured doubled faces for immortality. Then came an announcement of a lecture by a twin researcher, and the crowd flowed back into the big hall.

"Do you recognize the following situation?" asked the bearded man leaning on the lectern. "You're walking along

through the city minding your own business. Suddenly a
pretty girl you don't know comes up to you and throws her
arms around you. It doesn't happen very often, unless you
look like a famous star, or—you have a monozygotic twin
brother."

A murmur of acknowledgment filled the room, and
there were giggles.

The twin researcher went on. "Often it happens that
twins try to telephone one another at the same time and so
both get a busy signal." Heads also nodded at his statement
that sometimes twins will buy the same piece of clothing
on exactly the same day.

Then, however, the researcher dismissed such stories
somewhat scornfully as "twin folklore." Twin research
involves much more than funny and entertaining anec-
dotes. His voice became louder and more serious.

Siri felt as if she were in a confused dream. She searched
for the exit and heard only scraps of the lecture as she pressed
her way through the women, men, and children: "Genetics
on the one hand, and environmental influences on the
other . . . skin cancer . . . intelligence . . . environment influences the genotype . . . the phenotype is how a person
looks . . . anxiety patterns have a genetic foundation. . . . "

Oh, where was the door? Panic overwhelmed Siri as the
people began to clap. The crowd with its rhythmically
moving arms and hands seemed to want to hold her fast.
She pressed past bodies, wanted out of this doubled world
where everyone seemed to see with four eyes and smell with
two noses, and they tormented her with echoing sentences
out of doubled mouths:

—If my sister dies, I don't want to live a month longer.

—Everyone has always mixed us up, even in the maternity ward.

—We've been together for seventy-five years and have never fought.

—Suddenly there were two of them! What a shock!

—A double marriage with another pair of twins—that's what we dream of.

—I don't understand how they can dress so differently.

—My twin sister and I had our babies on the same day.

By the beginning of the next program item, entitled "Twins' Roundtable," which was to be followed by a musical group, The Twins and the Sheet Metal Boys, Siri was standing in the lobby. Finally she was alone. Only a dull murmur and laughter reached her through the big double doors. Dazed, she walked along the walls displaying artwork by pairs of twin artists.

I've never forgotten that color photo by an artist twin. Two red sweatsuits with *Chicago Bulls* across the chest were hanging on clothes hangers. The empty hoods stared at me like dead faces. The left suit had the right leg missing, and the right suit was missing the left one. Only together did they become two-legged and able to run.

The longer I looked at that picture, Iris, the more I saw and finally understood about me/you/us. Those two one-legged people were dependent on one another in the same way that we were. But you didn't just cut off one of my legs;

you took an arm and a hand too. You had everything and I had nothing.

The oneness of the pairs of twins who had come here was real. All were equally free or equally unfree. Real twins originate together, and one doesn't exist without the other. But the oneness act that you pulled was unreal. I was the copy and you were the original. You had me produced. You alone had the power. Without you, I wouldn't exist. I would never belong here.

All this twin bliss was unbearable. It had driven me out of the auditorium, and that was a good thing. Otherwise I might never have seen the photograph with the red sweatsuits.

After that weekend, Siri's gaze at Iris had changed and become pitiless. She dared to look carefully, and all at once she saw how much had changed in the recent weeks. Iris's hand trembled when she put her fork to her mouth. Food dropped from her lips, and she even spilled her coffee. When Iris stood, she skillfully levered herself up by exerting pressure on the back of the chair. Sometimes she tottered slightly when she went down the long hallway. Then she supported herself against the wall, where the white wallpaper was already becoming quite gray. Ashamed, Siri watched through the crack of the open bathroom door as her mother put on a diaper before a long meeting. Iris's beautiful round handwriting grew more and more angular and scribbly, and the once-so-perfect notations on the parchment sheets became distorted and unattractive.

As sad as all this was, Siri welcomed every change that

made her and Iris different. The MS seemed to her almost a lucky coincidence, for it strengthened the differences between the two: as Iris became sicker and older, the healthy Siri looked that much more radiant.

Siri felt her pity for Iris diminishing, but what she felt instead she didn't know. She was reeling through an emotional no-man's-land, unsteady in her feelings and in her nightly dreams.

In my nursery there hung a small wooden display case with a gorgeous blue Caligo butterfly. I often dreamed of seeing this butterfly sailing through the air with widestretched, dark-blue wings.

Now on the nightly stage in my head I was only a fat, unattractive caterpillar, which had to grow and wanted to change. Like a person pulling a shirt over her head, this animal shed one skin after another. But as many of these transparent skins as the caterpillar shed, it found no rest. It did not pupate, and it crawled around exhausted.

I could not change into a beautiful blue butterfly anymore, and I just ended up shriveled and disintegrating like that dumb, unhappy caterpillar.

Despairing, Siri looked for things she could hold onto, such as the picture with the sweatsuits. In those days there were no books or experts who could help the few existing clones understand themselves and the world better. And so, in her helplessness, Siri madly read everything she could find about twins. She learned to accept that she was one of them but came to know with even more certainty that clones were something different, not just artificially produced identical twins.

In not one of the countless books she read did she find a term that could describe this menacing otherness she felt. Then one day, entirely by accident, an article on a completely different subject came into her hands, and in an instant she understood what clone *really* meant.

You have made it much too simple, you singletons! Your idea is: A clone is the same as a twin. This idea prevailed for a long time, and not without purpose—after all, you couldn't be against clones if you were for twins. So if twins were produced in nature, it wasn't up to humans to forbid clones.

To make the mindless, unimaginative formula—that is, clone equals twin—attractive, there were even more exquisite arguments: The modern *I* might be understood to be in disintegration anyway. And so, since there was nothing more for anyone to rely on, it shouldn't matter if someone existed twice.

The word *clone* that was on everyone's tongue is a technical term, valueless and neutral. But I want to be moralistic, so I have created a moral word to spit at you: Don't talk anymore of cloning or of clones, talk of *misbreeding*.

This word resembles the word *misuse*, as in abuse, and that is exactly what's intended. For both are morally obscene, and the victims suffer similarly. Both don't understand for a long time what happened or is happening to them. They love the perpetrator, who exploits their trust. They withdraw from their environment and from others of their own age, as I have done. They feel they are to blame for everything that has happened to them, and they prefer to keep quiet about it. They so despise themselves that they hate their bodies; some go so far as to starve themselves almost to death or burn themselves with cigarettes. The abused cry silently for help—just like me when I got faint and banged my head on the piano keys.

Cloning is misbreeding—the word also has to translate so that even Mortimer G. Fisher can understand me, finally. How would *repro abuse* do?

Please don't ever talk about love again when the subject is cloning. Narcissus was looking for his dead twin sister when he admired his reflection, but not even he—the prototype of someone in love with himself—ever created a clone to order. Narcissus himself was never so high-handed and self-loving!

You who are engaged in this repro abuse are neither man nor woman but a third sex. The ancient Greeks recognized and described you in the myth of the god Eros, which tells how love between man and woman came into the world:

The male-female was one creature, all its extremities and sense organs doubled, and the round shape wheeled along, forceful and circling. This mighty sex now intended to break into heaven and attack the gods. To prevent this, Zeus cut the male-female being completely in half and formed one part into a man, the other a woman. Since then, each half has sought the other. Every human being is always seeking the other part, and that is what people call "eros" or "love." It is the attempt to return to the original state, and to make one out of two.

But cloners don't act out of love. They bring nothing together—rather, they split. Out of one they make two, or four, or eight. . . . Clones are the third sex of the third millennium; the cloner attacks the gods and intends to be the Creator itself.

For SHE spoke: Let me make a creature in my own image. In the name of the Mother, the Daughter, and the Holy Gene-Spirit.

And so I, Siri, came into the world as a misbreed.

To understand that and to give myself a label made me conscious of who I really was. This new clone consciousness gave me support, strengthened me, and made me give it some thought for the first time. Never again did I faint. I no longer hated my body, and I increasingly found myself beautiful. I knew who the guilty one was and began to hate my mother and her superior force.

Wherever I went or wanted to go, she blocked my way, and the way to Kristian too. Annoying obstacles are to be pushed aside. I realized that without her there would have been no me, but without her there would still be me, alone. My thoughts turned to lynch justice. And to kill you, Iris, would not be murder—it would be suicide, free of criminal penalty. They would find your fingerprints on the murder weapon, and there would be nothing to implicate me. The perfect crime.

My thoughts of murder frightened me so badly that for the next few weeks I was especially nice to the unsuspecting Iris.

One evening when Kristian called, Iris had gone to dinner with Thomas Weber and a music publisher, and so Siri answered the telephone. She said "Hello."

"Hello, Iris. This is Kristian. I'm back again. Can we get together?"

"Kristian, I've missed you." Without thinking about it, Siri turned into Iris. She had listened to some of Iris's conversations so often that she knew what to say to remain undetected.

She suggested to him that he come by on Saturday afternoon around five o'clock, since Siri would be out with Janeck. Kristian had his own house key, so she would wait for him in the bedroom. Waiting five days would be hard on him, said Kristian's gorgeous, sexy voice. But if it couldn't be any other way, then he would come on Saturday. Then he added, "I love you," and Siri's stomach did a thousand somersaults.

Her hand was trembling as she hung up. She was ashamed to have lied, but perhaps it had to be that way. Troubled, she sat down at Mr. Black and played for a long time, and more and more she took delight in the idea of again slipping completely into Iris's skin.

Siri was fidgety in the next few days. Her anticipation was mixed with fear—especially when the telephone rang—that Kristian might call and her deception would be discovered. And sometimes, when she looked at Iris, she blushed because she intended to deceive her so shamelessly.

"Are you coming down with something?" asked Iris, looking at her daughter with concern. "Do you have a fever?" She put her hand on Siri's forehead.

Siri escaped with a turn of her head and cracked, "Apparently there can be hot flashes in puberty too, and not just—"

"—during menopause," Iris finished with a laugh. "So you think I can go to Munich?"

"Absolutely. I'm not sick."

At night in bed, Siri thought only about Saturday. When Iris was at the studio in Munich meeting with a young pianist who was going to include some of her piano pieces on his new CD, Kristian would be with her. And while Iris was listening to her music in Munich, Siri and Kristian would be making love. She would be making love with a man for the first time, and she hoped it would be as wonderful as she always imagined in her daydreams.

He must have felt from the first moment that something wasn't right, although it was dark in the bedroom and I'd used your perfume and was wearing your negligée. He kissed me and stroked my breast, and immediately, as soon as he touched me, he wanted me. He must have noticed how firm my skin was and how I glowed. So he only wanted me, the young Iris, at that moment. I would certainly have pleased him better than you, I am very certain of that! He had that lustful look again. But then he lost his courage. When I tried to pull him toward the bed, he tore himself from my arms in the middle of the most marvelous kiss and turned on the light.

"Siri, that wasn't a good idea," he said. And even when I swore how much I was in love with him, he only shook his head. "It would be best if we just forget this," he said, "and

I won't say anything to Iris."

But he'd kissed me so lovingly just now! It was all Iris's fault! She spoiled everything. Certainly she'd forbidden him to kiss me like that—she didn't intend to share him, wouldn't even grant me this first love. And she would have to pay for that!

I demanded that Kristian never show his face at our house again. Otherwise I'd say that he'd dragged me to bed, utterly shamelessly. Just the way he'd kissed me. "And I know," I added, "that Iris would believe me and tell *you* to go to hell. You can be sure of that. She doesn't miss how you always look at me. So you'd better disappear."

Kristian saw that I was serious. He tried to say something else, but I wouldn't let him get a word out. "You're a miserable coward," I said, and I wrapped myself in Iris's negligée and left the room. He didn't run after me when I went down the hall slowly, didn't take me in his arms again. I lay down on my bed and waited. My heart beat faster when I heard his steps, but they got farther away. And when the front door closed, I cried with disappointment and angrily pounded the pillow.

In the days and weeks that followed, I ran for the telephone when it rang, but I never heard Kristian's voice again.

Love troubles hurt especially badly when there's no one to share them with or comfort you.

When Siri was sitting across from her mother, she would sometimes wonder how Kristian had made love to her. Siri was disgusted by her thoughts, but she wasn't able to get rid of the picture in her head. Iris and Siri had become rivals.

"Are you having love troubles? Could you be in love?" Iris asked suddenly when they were eating together one evening.

"Who with? Everything between Janne and me is the same as ever!"

"Perhaps there's a new admirer?" asked Iris.

Siri acted indifferent. "Where'd you get that idea?"

One of our favorite operas had been *The Valkyrie*, by Richard Wagner. In the first act Sieglinde recognizes the man with whom she has fallen in love as her twin brother Siegmund, and she rejoices: "When my eye fell upon you, you were my own." You always pressed my hand at this spot. Filled with emotion, and because the music was so gorgeous, I had tears in my eyes, just like you.

Siegmund and his sister make love in the forest, in defiance of all laws. The fruit of their twin incest is a boy called Siegfried. His birth is the beginning of the twilight of the gods, when the old gods and their laws lose their powers.

To have yourself cloned is not only repro abuse. It's also incest: genetic and emotional incest. And so in the end, we clones—perhaps because we have two lives and are bad by nature—deprive those who have created us of power. We ring in the twilight of the mothers and fathers.

I wanted to topple you, Iris! I had not been able to steal Kristian from you, and my colorful clothes hadn't bothered you for a long time. I had to destroy you with your own instrument and become the better pianist. But in your delusion of omnipotence, you thought I would do everything only *for* you.

Iris Sellin had a new composition ready. *Echoes II* was to be performed for the first time at Siri's first big solo evening. The interpreter would also play several drums and a glockenspiel, and at the end play a toy piano.

"That's meant as an ironic commentary," Iris explained.

"Ridiculous!" Siri felt she was being mocked. "Is that supposed to be me, the toy piano? Well, I'm certainly not going to play this piece." For the first time they argued fiercely over one of Iris's compositions.

"Get hold of yourself," Iris said when Siri refused to play even one note of *Echoes II* and threatened to forget the concert altogether.

"How can I get hold of myself when I never had a self of my own?" Siri sneered. How she hated that all-knowing tone!

"Siri, what's this about? There's no reason to act this way. Are you nervous because the rehearsal time is so short? Don't worry, child, we still have three months to prepare the concert."

"Damn it, I'm fifteen and haven't been a child for a long time. Ask Kristian, why don't you!" Siri was out to hurt Iris.

"What do you mean by that?" Iris asked guardedly.

"Ask him yourself."

"But he's not back in Lübeck yet."

"He's been back since last month. Didn't he call you?" Siri acted very surprised.

"And how do you know that he's back?" Iris watched

her daughter mistrustfully. When she saw Siri's left eyebrow twitching, she knew that Siri was keeping something from her.

"Have you slept with him?" Iris had scarcely said the words when she was appalled at the question and at her jealousy.

"I don't have to tell you."

Siri's snippy answer provoked Iris. "You little sneak!" she hissed. "He's twice your age."

"As if that made any difference. He's ten years younger than you. You're welcome to have him back anyway. He's not really so good in bed. Or maybe we should share him? One week be a turn for YouI, and then a week for Iyou."

"You little monster!" Iris gave her daughter a resounding slap on the cheek, and she was immediately appalled. She'd reacted exactly as her mother would have.

"I guess that makes you the monster-mother," Siri said scornfully, and she stood up and left the room.

When the door slammed shut, Iris wept with rage because she'd lost her self-control over a man. He must not be allowed to come between her and Siri. Nothing would separate them, and certainly not a dumb infatuation. But she would not go after Siri now. After all, she was Taiwo and Siri was only Kehinde. And she would come to her senses again. Siri always worked like crazy getting ready for a concert.

Music is longing, you said once. What were you longing for when you composed me? Immortality? Why do you compose? This question is often asked of you makers of modern music. Today I'm asking you for the last time: Why did you compose me? A, T, G, C are discordant notes, and the harmonies of DNA hurt in my soul. They hurt in your soul too.

Iris slept badly—she was sorry about the slap. And so around two o'clock she got up, went to Siri's bedroom, and sat down beside her daughter's bed. Until now she'd always found peace there, and at the sight of her clone she'd felt certain that everything was good about it, everything was right.

But that night when Iris looked at Siri's young face, she brooded over when and where Kristian might have betrayed her with Siri. Her daughter must almost have been compelled to fall in love with him. After all, what pleased Iris pleased Siri just the same. One heart and one soul. Suddenly she felt tears in her eyes.

But what if two people could not live *one* life? One of them had better disappear, and of course it should be the one with the least life in her. It would be the most logical thing to administer the mercy shot to the twin who was old and sick. Or should she kill the young Iris before she too became ill with MS and was broken by the great task of having to replay Iris's life once more? The black thoughts circled faster and faster, and they swept Iris along with them. A strange, powerful feeling flooded over her. Tears no longer blurred her sight, and now there was only naked hatred.

I peeped through my closed eyelids and watched you while

you thought I was sleeping. When I saw that fathomless hatred in your eyes, I finally felt I was whole, and I felt it with every fiber of my body. I rejoiced inwardly, for now I was someone. Finally you were taking me seriously. For the first time I moved out of you and was standing opposite you, Iris. The duel could begin.

Duel
Youth II

Why do you singletons fear us? Maybe because we are more than doppelgängers, ghostly doubles. And this "more" makes you uneasy. Maybe there's something lurking in us clones that will ultimately make us the victors over the singletons. Maybe that's the small compensation for our early defathering or demothering. In any case, I felt this "more" as I prepared myself for my first big solo concert. I wanted to defeat Iris, not substitute for her. To not only be as good as she was, but better. Much better!

It was not—at least not only—the youthful audacity of a sixteen-year-old that made me feel that way. It was the clone in me: Even at the very beginning—I'm now firmly convinced of it—it had already sucked up all the knowledge of the thirty-two-year-old Iris-life into itself. And the interpretation of music ultimately comes down to life experience. What could happen to me? I had this "more," and I was also younger, healthier, and more attractive than Iris. My gorgeous blue concert gown, clinging elegantly around my hips, would captivate everyone, and my playing would draw them all under its spell. Before the concert, I felt I was so beautiful and so strong, and I believed in myself more firmly than I had ever before in my life.

The applause was polite and brief. When Siri stepped forward to bow, she sought and found Dada's and Janeck's faces. She held on to their smiles so she wouldn't collapse.

Iris Sellin sat in a wheelchair between Thomas Weber and a well-known music critic. Iris avoided Siri's searching, anxious gaze and felt herself just as humiliated as her twin. What was supposed to have been a triumph had been not even a mediocre performance but a defeat, a disgrace.

Siri had played worse and worse, with leaden fingers and limbs and an empty head. She had struck colorless notes like a wind-up doll, and the music had degenerated to a lifeless accumulation of notes.

I was torn, as happens to any good interpreter: She should always follow the composer's text to the very letter while also obeying the mood of the moment and her feelings. Otherwise, her playing never comes alive. Every pianist is a commercial property in the concert market, but even so she should be an independent personality—slave and rebel at the same time. That is what makes her value increase.

The piece of music that I was supposed to perform was called *Your Life*, and I tried to play it as *My Life*. I wanted the applause for me alone. But in the end I was only a marionette that dangled on your DNA strands, Iris. And that night they got tangled up. The marionette didn't move right, so I only played the notes on the page.

No, Iris, stage fright was not to blame—that's too simple. It was the contradictory expectations of you and of me. Iyou and YouI were alternately whispering different instructions in my ear. They confused me and I no longer heard what I was playing. The voices kept at me, but one thing won the upper hand in this confusion and became louder and louder, and that, Iris, was your/my/our mocking laughter.

Iris had counted along on every beat—for her, too, the minutes to the final chord had stretched into a torturing eternity.

Iris was ashamed for her daughter who had so failed so miserably. She had to keep herself from crying out in help-lessness, for she wanted to comfort her child and at the same time curse the clone off the stage.

The blue dress rustled as Siri bowed. She was hot and cold and sweating. She was certain that dark spots were showing under her arms. She was ashamed. She would have preferred to run into Dada's arms, but she quickly bowed once more to avoid the looks.

In hundreds of eyes there was the same look. They stabbed me with their looks like an insect. They killed me to look at me from all sides in a glass case—like my beloved blue Caligo butterfly.

We twins were always the exception to the rule. In earlier times they killed us or left us out to die like Romulus and Remus. Siamese twins served either as amusements or curiosities, ending up in circus acts, or filling the shelves of anatomy laboratories as specimens preserved in alcohol.

The modern times viewed twins as "experiments of life." These "living laboratories" were studied to help to understand the indivisible, the individual. And so in Nazi concentration camps pairs of twins were inoculated and compared, observed and measured, tortured and dismembered. What makes up a human being—race, talent, or personality? Perhaps twins hold the answer, and so we will breed clones.

Up there on the stage I was nothing more than a pitiful exhibit. No listener had come to this concert to hear me play the music. They only gaped at the clone of Iris Sellin, comparing her and me. I heard the singletons down there in the concert hall whispering and maligning me. "Monster," they hissed, just the way Oma Katharina had hissed "monster."

The pained applause ebbed as Siri stiffly walked off the stage. Then the audience all rose from their seats as if at a secret sign and turned toward Iris Sellin. The applause swelled anew. The public would not be fobbed off with this copy. It wanted the real Sellin, the only one, the true one.

"Play!" demanded one voice, then a chorus of voices. "Play, play, play!"

Iris was surprised and overwhelmed. Thomas Weber

talked to her while her eyes looked for Siri, but she had already left the stage. The critic bent toward her and asked, "May I push you to the stage?" Iris nodded.

He pushed Iris up a small ramp and onto the stage very close to the piano. People sat down, and the hall grew quiet. With sick hands, Iris played what the public expected: passages from *Echoes* and *Dewdrops*. She let chords from her operas sound and she enchanted them with her setting of the troubadour song, "When Tears of Joy Flow."

Iris's playing was worse than her daughter's, but no one heard it, because no one wanted to hear it. The aura of the original clouded their senses. As with a picture, a copy—however perfect—never outshines the original.

You should not have done that to me, Motwi. Backstage, I heard the clapping of people who were hungry for uniqueness. They were right, of course. No human being can be *repeated*—that word sounds and is just as absurd as I am myself.

My whole body was trembling, and I held my ears to not have to hear that swelling applause, which only you, the original, were worthy of. I felt small and miserable and betrayed by you, a good-for-nothing misbreed!

Then suddenly Janeck was standing beside me. It wasn't you, Iris, though I'd been waiting for you. He, not you, took me in his arms to comfort me.

"Janne, let's drive to the shore," I pleaded, "just for a few days."

I could not face you again so soon, Iris.

Slowly I moved to the backstage door. I kept hoping you

would look for me and find me. But probably I had played too badly to keep being your life.

The music critics were restrained. Many even wrote almost unbearably understandingly about Siri's "debut." The pressure of expectation had been too high, no wonder with this mother, whose "moving appearance" was given more space by most than the real concert. That was at least something special, after all, something for the spirit. They attributed the failure of Siri Sellin to a "bad day" and stage fright. However, one journalist wrote a mercilessly devastating review under the headline, "Fuzzy Blueprint—Siri Sellin's First Concert Disappoints All."

"At least he took me seriously. The others only pitied me," said Siri when Janeck read her the reviews. He called it his "face-up-to-reality training."

As they sat together in chairs at the beach, Janeck asked Siri, "Will you perform again? Do you want to try it again?"

"Perhaps," was her hesitant answer.

Siri could not imagine a life without music and without concerts, without Iris and Mr. Black. Iris, the enchantress of sounds, had woven a spell around her. But Siri asked herself more and more often: What would life be like out there, outside the boundaries? Without her, in freedom?

"You can move in with me anytime. I still have the little room that I can clear out," Janeck said. "Hamburg is so much better than Lübeck. There's more going on. It's a city that can turn your mind to other thoughts. And maybe you'll finally fall in love with the right one." Full of persuasive power, he beamed at Siri.

"You're the right one, but the right brother," said Siri carefully.

"Well, of course. That's a promise forever and ever. Separate yourself from her at last, and I'm your no-matter-what-happens brother."

"I don't know if I can do that." Siri looked thoughtful and dug her toes into the cool sand.

"You have to do it." Janeck took his sister by the hand and together they walked along the beach. As Siri felt the sea breeze on her skin, her head finally grew light and free.

The two of them could laugh now over the expression *fuzzy blueprint*. It had been witty, at least, Janeck said. Why did she have to wear that blue dress too? He grinned. "But that dress, at least that was sharp."

Siri picked up a jellyfish lying on the beach and threw it at Janeck, who swiftly moved his head out of the line of fire and cried, "If you want to move in with me, you have to get used to throwing things."

For several days after the debacle, Iris's brain could not bring together what her eyes saw. It was laughable that double pictures tormented her when her doppel-gänger wasn't even there. Now, all by herself, she could play the YouI-Iyou game that Siri didn't want to play any-more. But this was a solo cast with no young Iris. The two mirror images were old and sick and made everything doubly desolate.

When Daniela Hausmann told her of the young people's trip, Iris had been glad to be alone and not to have to face Siri. She knew only too well how her own performance must have shamed her daughter. But Iris had also wanted the applause, applause like the old days, a small consolation. For recently she'd been forcefully made aware of how much she was losing control of her body.

Iris no longer dared to leave the house on her own after she'd twice fallen in the street. People had meanly commented on her uncertain, staggering gait and the falls: "She's drunk!" or "She should be ashamed of herself, going around like that in broad daylight!" After these humiliating experiences, Iris decided to use only the wheelchair on the street. She released a public statement that she was suffering from MS and so could no longer give concert performances. But she would try to keep composing as long as possible.

Iris hated pity, and she kept secret even from Siri how much strength the least effort cost her. More and more nerve conduits were broken or disturbed by inflammatory foci. On some days Iris thought she could actually hear where these cable fires were flaming up and crackling destructively. Her thoughts tangled like yarn, and she could not find a beginning or an end to them. From time to time the thoughts even tore in two. She looked for the connections, but she no longer knew anything then. She forgot things. When Iris wanted to write down her music, she could hardly make the pen hit the lines. Daniela helped her, writing everything in a clear hand. And now this concert, on top of it all! The excitement made her hands and legs tremble even more.

The medications, her music, and being alone were good for Iris, and she slowly recovered. The flare of the disease subsided and the double vision disappeared. And the better she felt, the angrier she became with Janeck. He was the interference factor, she persuaded herself. He was alienating Siri from her. Once again she must cut him out and prepare a wonderful present for her daughter. And so Iris undertook to compose a new piece of music.

You were no longer seeing clearly and no longer had enough strength for our duel, Iris. You longed only for rest. And so a flute, a clarinet, a string quartet, and a piano tell the story of the Sellin twins, who find each other again in Terra Lonhdana, a faraway country where peace reigns. Laboriously you sought the notes that you felt and you succeeded in bringing a painful longing to utterance. Was it the longing for your clone, for a new life? Or was it also a longing for death? You expressed all your heartache in this composition. You probably sensed that *Terra Lonhdana* would be your last work. But never that it would bring us to the very last time that I would play for you in our life!

Siri came back a week later. They both told one another what they'd been doing the previous week. Both carefully avoided speaking about the concert.

But then Iris laid some old newspaper clippings on the table. "I dug these out for you. Just read what bad reviews I got at the beginning. I had exactly the same experience you did. Stage fright made me play like an automaton. That happens to everyone and you can't give up now. You have to keep practicing, and the next time—"

"It wasn't stage fright," said Siri. "And whether there'll be a next time, I don't know."

"Of course there'll be a next time." Iris laid her hand on Siri's shoulder. "I'll help you. I know how much that hurt."

"You don't know how much it hurt *me*." Siri turned away, not wanting Iris to touch her.

"I've been working on a new composition, especially for us. Will you play it for me?" Iris asked. And Siri nodded.

It was the first sunny Sunday in May, and the bright spring light poured into the music room as Siri sat down in front of Mr. Black. As always she stroked the shining black wood in greeting. With a start, she heard rubber wheels squeaking slightly on the parquet. Her mother had never used the wheelchair in the apartment before. Iris Sellin stretched herself up in her chair, and on the music rack placed the note-covered pages she'd fetched from her large work table.

"Are you feeling so much worse?" Siri asked.

"It isn't so bad. I can't stand long, though, and all the to-ing and fro-ing this morning has made me tired. Purely a cautionary measure." Iris spread the pages smooth. "I'm eager to know how you like it."

Siri adjusted the piano stool and opened the keyboard cover, then read the title of the piano arrangement.

"What does Terra Lonhdana mean?" she asked.

"Distant Land," Iris answered.

"That sounds sad."

"Perhaps, but only a little. Please play, Siri! You're still my life."

You should not have said that. Not at that moment! After the horrendous concert, the line no longer seemed to me like a curse, but like pure mockery. But you didn't even notice! I looked at the black keys, which combined like twins and triplets. I placed my arms in the correct playing posture, then my hands. They were mirror images, and the thumbs moved on the center axis.

Were these mirrored things actually my hands? When I tried to strike the first notes, my fingers would not obey, as if they no longer belonged to me. Exactly—they were also Iris's hands. How was I supposed to play with these hands? And where had my own disappeared to? Where I had just seen them, great black holes in the keys swallowed them up.

"They're gone," I stammered. "I can't see my hands anymore."

Full of panic, I turned around to you and cried, "Help!"

You also cried out, and you rolled your wheelchair forward so fast that it bumped against Mr. Black and the arm rest scraped a deep scratch in the black wooden frame.

"Move your fingers. It's only a cramp. You haven't been practicing enough! Try it!" you implored me.

But I could not play. My hands stayed vanished.

"Play anyhow, just play!" You tugged on me, panic and fear on your face. Then you let go of me and rolled into the next room.

At this moment we were both thinking the same thing: Your child is having the first attack of MS and you're to blame. You passed this damned disease to your daughter.

Finally you had Thomas Weber on the phone. "Siri's

sick. You have to get her to the doctor immediately," she commanded him.

I kept staring at the keys on either side of the black holes. The funny thing was, I suddenly was no longer afraid but felt free. I was still sitting in a cage, but the door was open. My hands had been the first to leave. They'd simply flown away.

I ought to take this event seriously, warned the doctor in the clinic where I was kept for observation for one day. He also said that the black holes I'd described could probably be explained as symptoms of an ocular migraine. That was not so uncommon after overexertion or conditions of extreme anxiety and tension.

I felt so light without my hands. And since without them I could no longer play, there was also no longer any reason to stay with you. I could no longer make you healthy that way.

"Don't throw everything away! We'll get through it together!" Iris begged her daughter when she was back home again.

"I can get through it alone," said Siri determinedly.

"I know, but—"

"I don't want to know anymore what you know!" screamed Siri. "You always know everything about me. You think you know everything. But I'm not you, understand that once and for all!"

Siri stormed into the music room and her mother laboriously followed her with a walker. She heard how the keyboard cover slammed down and Siri beat on Mr. Black with her fists and kicked at the legs of the concert grand.

Iris Sellin stopped in the open doorway of the music room. "He really can't do anything about it," she said, forcing herself to maintain her composure. Just don't scream! she commanded herself. "You need a few days rest. Then we'll try it again, Siri. We'll start all over again. And you'll see, we'll manage. But today I have to go to a meeting with my music publisher. I'll have Thomas pick me up a little earlier. I'm sure you'll want to be alone." She sought and found Siri's grayish blue eyes. "Two are always stronger than one. I love you twice as much, Youl."

"You can drop that little game! I'm not a child, and I haven't been for a long time."

Iris made no reply and turned the walker around. Her feet dragged across the wooden floor.

When Iris had left the apartment, Siri went through all the rooms. She stretched out full length under the protecting belly of Mr. Black and stroked the scratches on the wooden legs. "I'm sorry," she murmured.

The hallway that led to her room had never seemed so long to her. Siri packed two suitcases. Then she telephoned Janeck and told him that she would be arriving at the Hamburg main station at 4:45, without a return ticket.

Kehinde no longer wanted to follow Taiwo. When the apartment door closed behind me, I made up for the cry that I had not made at my birth. Every human being cries at the beginning of his life, except I hadn't. And so now I screamed that much louder, for I felt as if I were newborn. Luckily the street was entirely empty.

From the bus that took her to the train station, Siri saw the tower of St. Peter's church with its high point and the four little corner towers. Perhaps her wish note was still hanging up there in the vaulting, the paper already yellowed and the ink faded. And Siri wept, because all the wishes had been in vain: She would not become a great pianist, she had never seen Kristian, her first love, again, and she hadn't fallen in love with anyone afterward. That tickling feeling when she looked through the opening in the vaulting or looked at Kristian seemed to have been lost to her forever. So the tears ran down her face for that reason too.

Our free will is still the most wonderful biological attainment! All the damned genes can go to hell. We *can* change ourselves if we really want to. I started with what was easiest: First I painted my room at Janeck's black and blue, including all the furniture. Iris had only allowed white walls. Then I started on my appearance. And because I was convinced that the external also influences our inner life, I was very radical. I had my hair cut ultrashort, colored it raven black, and eventually put some fiery red streaks in it. I changed my eye color with some brown contact lenses.

I practiced new gestures and movements in front of the mirror. Away with that Sellin walk, away with those head movements when I laughed and the slight wrinkling of the nose. I painted my mouth dark red and wore even more wildly colored, glaringly bright clothes than before. Only one thing mattered: Everything had to be different.

"Normally people do that when they're twelve or thirteen years old," Janeck teased, "but go ahead and break out. It's about time. Just please don't skip too much school!"

I was sixteen when I got drunk for the first time, to the point that I got sick. I went dancing with Janeck and his crowd, and because I was musical, I very quickly learned to move in time to the strange rhythms. I slept with a man for the first time, a friend of Janne's who was ten years older than I. He made it easy and lovely for me, but I did not fall in love with him. It was a kind of obligatory program that I was carrying out. I worked through one point of "normal life" after another—or those things I thought were normal. But nothing gave me much pleasure. That's a problem with free will—it can't solve everything either, and we lose power over it, especially at night.

In my dreams I gave concerts again and wallowed in the applause. And whenever I dreamed of Iris, I was certain the next morning that she also had seen me in her sleep. I missed Mr. Black and Iris so much that I cried into my pillow with homesickness like a little child, and Janeck had to comfort me. I should just call Iris, he advised me when he saw how I was suffering.

Never, I said. This time she has to follow me. And I functioned, forced myself to go to school regularly and learned almost mechanically. But I was really waiting for you, Iris! You were supposed to come and rescue me from this nightmare.

Siri won the test of strength. After two months Iris called and suggested a discussion. Siri insisted that she come to Hamburg, although Janeck's apartment was on the fifth floor and there was no elevator. She knew that Iris could only climb stairs with the greatest effort, but Siri was too afraid of succumbing to the spell of the twin island again. Here with Janne, who promised to wait for her in his room, she felt more secure. Here the carefully cultivated protective armor would better withstand the concentrated twin love. Iris proposed to come by the very next day at around six in the evening. Thomas Weber would drive her there.

Siri hardly slept that night, not only because it was a rare hot spell in July. She kept rehearsing the impending scene: How Iris's eyes would widen with dismay at the sight of her daughter, and what she wanted to say to her.

Iris came very punctually. When Siri opened the door, Iris looked as stunned as her daughter had hoped. She was speechless, and she kept her tears back only with great difficulty. That repaid Siri for the many tears she had shed in her loneliness.

"Do you recognize me, Iris?" she asked in her sharp-sounding new voice. Iris could not even nod, she was so shocked.

After they sat down at the big kitchen table, Siri gave Iris a glass of mineral water, which she drank greedily.

"Don't worry, Motwi, I'm still your genotype," said Siri. "Only the external influences have changed slightly. Don't you like this new phenotype at all? Siri as a brilliantly colored Iris-mishmash!" She grinned. "I've learned your lessons well. Music begins between order and chaos, you said once. But life also begins between order and chaos. Right now I'm living through chaos. I have to make up for a lot. Genetic history isn't predictable after all—even clones can be unpredictable and not like anyone else. You were wrong there. I'm a mistake."

"You are not unlike anyone else and you are not a mistake," said Iris almost lovingly.

"Yes, I am, and I was from the very beginning. Why am I alive, anyway? Tell me honestly for once." Siri sounded hard. "But why should I ask you what I've known for a long time. It wasn't love that brought me into the world. That kind of dumb love was beneath your dignity. You wanted to be entirely safe, so there was this damned incest!"

"But I do love you. You're being unfair," whispered Iris, and she dropped her head.

"Was what you did right, then? Was it right for me? I am a calculated person, predictable from the start. You subjected me to *your* life's program. *Your* life's program determined everything."

"But Siri, did it make you so unhappy? Was it so bad that I wanted you and gave you every opportunity? Every human being seeks himself in another, that's love. It could be so beautiful, just when you're getting older and beginning to understand everything better. These crises happen with all parents and children, not just us.

"Maybe clones only live in crises."

"Stop making everything ridiculous," said Iris. "The victim role doesn't suit you!"

"Do you know what's really ridiculous?" Siri bent toward her mother. "For a long time I thought Professor

Fisher was my real father."

"Siri, that *is* laughable. I was always honest with you. I never lied to you."

"Oh, yes, you lied to me, because you concealed from me what sort of a monster pair we are. Gaped at and wondered at by all! This lust that people have to see your clone fail—you said nothing about that to me. You didn't prepare me for that! And when it happened, you left me alone. And even worse, you played for them."

Iris tried to stay calm. "That was wrong, I know, but Siri, listen to me—"

"No, I don't want to listen to you anymore." Siri would not let her mother finish and covered her ears. "From now on I'm only listening to me. And the one sentence above all I never want to hear again: You are my life, you are my life. . . . "

Iris grew louder. "But remember the beautiful times! I gave you everything—love and talent and encouragement. You were content and happy. And what did you do with it? You threw it all away. Not only that, you made it bad. You're, damn it, an ungrateful— " Iris barely managed to swallow the word she was about to say.

"Creature!" screamed Siri. "Is the word sticking in your throat? Don't you dare say the truth? Are you afraid of your creature, this unsuccessful misbreed? Is it choking you? Will it kill you in the end?"

Siri's face twisted, and suddenly she was holding the fruit knife against Iris's throat. She didn't know how it got into her hand. A second ago it had been lying in the bowl with the apples.

"Siri, don't, please!" Iris implored.

It was still for a moment, then the knife loudly struck the floor. Siri breathed deeply.

"Didn't it turn out the way you planned it, this creature?" she asked her mother. "Do you plan to just discard it eventually? Maybe you still have a replacement waiting in the deep freeze?" Siri's voice was scornful.

"There's only you. Please stop. . . . "

"Too bad! Because there's always another level. I could have carried the third one. Looky, here come the Sellin triplets."

Iris remembered her mother's words: "She'll destroy you. In any case, she is even more heartless." Everything she wanted to say tangled into a snarl in her head. And so Siri did not learn how very much Iris loved her, or how sorry she was that everything had turned out this way. Iris only stammered, "Why are you so mean?"

She sounded so helpless and miserable, and she sat there looking so caved in, that Siri fell silent.

"It's all too much," Iris wept. "I can't think clearly anymore. The MS is destroying my brain. I can't compose anymore. Don't leave me. I have only you."

Siri was unyielding, although seeing Iris this way cut her to the heart.

"When I needed you, you were never there," she accused Iris. "You locked me out, even though I pounded on your door. You were never there when I was sick. Why should I stay with you now? I'm like you, after all, so I act exactly like you. Heartless. At least in this way I'm a complete success!"

"I'd like to go now," Iris said. "It's pointless for us to just scream at each other. Perhaps we could talk some other time, in Lübeck?"

Siri didn't answer. Silently she took Iris to the door. When she saw how laboriously her mother went down the stairs, she quickly shut the door.

I almost became Kehinde again, almost ran down the stairs and followed you. Only when the door closed was I safe from you.

I waited behind the curtain until I heard an engine start, and I knew Thomas Weber's car had pulled away. Then I opened the window and watched the vehicle until it disappeared around the corner.

I didn't cry because I didn't want to cry. But I didn't feel like the victor in this duel, either. I was just wretched. When I heard Janeck's steps in the hall, I felt better again. No, I wasn't alone. But you, Iris, were! And it served you right.

SHE had elevated herself above all, and it's lonely up there. Being a goddess has a high price.

For Siri's seventeenth birthday Janeck gave her an easel, brushes, and paints. "Just try it," he said. "Colors are something like notes. Lots of people see music in colors. And a picture is a composition, just like a piece of music."

When Siri began to paint, she rediscovered her hands. Suddenly she loved her sturdy fingers. They could grip, and they were just right for stretching canvases, mixing colors, and guiding the big brush.

It was only several days later that Siri retrieved the large package from the bureau, which had lain there unopened since her birthday. Iris had sent it to her. It contained the original manuscript of *Dewdrops* and nothing else, not even a note. Iris and Siri had not seen one another since Iris's visit. Siri did not respond to Iris's messages on the answering machine. But from Dada she learned that Iris's condition had worsened in the three months since her visit.

Siri took the *Dewdrops* manuscript and, page by page, cut and folded and stuck the lines of notes together in new ways. She painted over this collage with vigorous, broad black and blue brushstrokes, circles, and curlicues. As she painted, her movements followed the rhythms of the music she had known since her life began, and that she still always heard in her innermost thoughts.

The Sellin twins often met in my daydreams. We had to appear together, of course—we'd become a sought-after circus attraction.

"Everybody! Everybody, step right up!" intoned the barker. "Come see the Siamese twins Siri and Iris, the two-headed musician with four hands!

We've just made our entrance. Quiet, it's the barker's turn again.

"May I have your attention, Ladies and Gentlemen! The monster show is beginning. Today we offer you a worldwide sensation, the Siamese twins of the twenty-first century. Let's have lights for our clone pair! Heh, heh, heh,

no, not these two clowns—I said *clones!* C-L-O-N-E-S.
Let's have some applause for our clone pair, Siri and Iris!

"Note the skillful choice of names and the similarity
from head to toe. Did you know that identical twins not
only have the same fingerprints, they have the same brain
waves too? Sometimes you can see flashes between their
heads. Danger, high voltage! Thought transference! Don't
get too near 'em. Are they man or machine?

"While Siri and Iris walk around the ring—yes, you can
touch 'em, folks—I'll fill you in on the story of the original
Siamese twins, Chang and Eng. These brothers—who were
attached from breastbone to navel—were born in Siam, the
modern Thailand, in the year eighteen hundred and
eleven. They traveled all through America as circus sensa-
tions. Each married a woman and each fathered several
children. After Chang died, his brother Eng followed him a
few weeks later. But they still live on in name!

"You, Ladies and Gentlemen, are about to witness an
exciting duel. Are these twins individuals or not? Separable
or inseparable? These are the great questions here. Listen
while Iris and Siri play something for us: with four hands
and one head, or with two hands and two heads, or even
four hands and the other head —anything's possible.

"Please observe the psychic bond. It's strong, yet it's
wrapped loosely around the necks of our two pianists. No,
to the woman in the first row, it is not an umbilical cord.
These bonds are made of a different, far more durable and
flexible stuff—clone-twin love.

"Each has now taken her place at the concert grand
piano, still bound with this thin, almost invisible bond.

With each chord the concert pianos will roll away from each other, and the bond will be snapped. But there is a potentially lethal risk! If the separation does not take place at the right moment, our artists could strangle themselves. Or would they split down the middle? Heh, heh, heh!

"The famed Iris Sellin will play excerpts from her own compositions *Echoes* and *Dewdrops*. The no less famed Siri Sellin will improvise on them. You, Ladies and Gentlemen, are witnesses to this world premiere. What is ordinarily a bloody procedure, attempted only in operating rooms, a procedure that often fails, we are going to resolve today with a concert. We're putting our money on the power of music!

"May I ask for your silence please. At my signal, the very first complete separation of the Siamese twins of the future will begin. Ready, clones, go!

"The first chord sounds. The psychic rope stretches. It's getting tighter . . . and tighter. Who will stop breathing first? Iris or Siri? Iris rears up. The younger Siri strikes the chords without mercy. Her piano leaps. But wait—something is happening on the other side. Iris is using her entire repertoire of skills: cascades, chords, trills. The bond is stretched to the breaking point, but it's still holding.

"Siri is turning blue. Don't worry—you there in the first row, sit back down in your seat—you won't see any blood. These bonds are bloodless. Are we close to a decision? Yes, yes—the bond is tearing. Bravo! But what's this? Iris Sellin slides from the piano stool. She seems to have stopped breathing! Please, don't panic, folks! Let our assistant carry her out of the ring. An emergency medic is standing by.

"Let's have some applause, Ladies and Gentlemen, for

this exciting, breathtaking duel. And the winner is . . . Siri Sellin, who bows, laughing."

I hid myself from her in Hamburg. But I couldn't escape her. When she became even sicker, pity drew me back to her. Love is stronger than reason, and clone love subdues any free will. As year nineteen began, my/your/our double life took me prisoner again.

Double Life
The Second Year Zero

You singletons certainly can split hairs when it has to do with us clones. Long before I was born, a jurist offered these shrewd arguments against our prohibition—that is, *for* our existence: "If, some day in the future, a human clone is asked if he would prefer not to have been cloned, he will reject the question as irrelevant. . . . For a clone, the alternatives are not 'cloned or not cloned', but 'cloned or nonexistent'."

Wherever did you get this damned conviction that we would rather be cloned than dead? Don't be so naive and judge us blueprints by you. Because you have something that we doubled creatures will never have: that absolute certainty of being an "I." This certain knowledge is not based on rational consideration, it's just there. Deep inside you, from the very beginning, it's there without your having to think about it. You see and feel this "I" as soon as you perceive the world and it perceives you. You inhale the certainty of being unique every second of your life. The clone has no "I."

I was always only she: Iris read backwards, a creature by her favor. I saw myself like someone who unscrews a giant Russian doll. Each doll inside looks just like the ones before, only the wooden shells get smaller and smaller, until at the end there's nothing more there. And that nothing was me.

No one can stand being a nothing for very long. I held out for half a year, but then on a cold, clear January day I got on the train and rode back to Lübeck. I had to see Iris because I didn't feel like myself anymore.

Blueprints are true, true blue. There's a little blue flower called forget-me-not. Forget-me-never! Or else you'll die, my life!

When we embraced each other in Lübeck on my first visit after I'd fled, it was as if she and I were grown together into this one being that rolled forward like a ball. And if either half wanted or had to go in a different direction—one toward life, the other toward death—this creature would stand still. I had no more strength to defend myself. I stood motionless, but there was no peace in this standstill, only despair. At that moment I regretted having come back, and I wanted to run away again. But my leaden feet would not move. I knew this unmoving-as-if-rooted-to-the-spot state from a dream in which I, like Iris, had sat in a wheelchair, but it had no wheels.

I kept tearing myself away from her and returning to Hamburg, to Janeck. And when I thought about her, a panicky fear came over me. Iris's lingering illness brought my life to a halt too.

Janne had not known what to do next, and his worry about Siri grew. "Neurotic depression" was the judgment of a psychologist whom Janeck asked for advice. Such behavior is not uncommon when a close relative is chronically ill, the specialist explained. But in this case everything was exacerbated. The sick person was, after all, Siri's mother *and* her twin. It didn't surprise him that, in such a situation, she was developing increasingly strong feelings of guilt. She was still healthy, and through her sympathy, she was almost suffering for the other one.

"What can I do?" asked Janeck.

"Just be there for her. That can do a great deal."

Janeck had been there for her the whole time. He'd done all the housework and seen to it that she got to school on time. He'd taken her to parties and art shows. Siri stood around, made conversation, but nothing and no one could reach her or touch her. Only when she was painting did her face relax. At those times, Janne could find his little sister again, with whom he had taken the forbidden scouting trips and had sat in beach chairs at the edge of the sea.

But now Siri was drifting away from Janeck too. When she wasn't in school or visiting her mother, she preferred to lie on her bed and hold silent dialogue for hours at a time with a picture on the wall. Once Janeck had taken it down when she wasn't home, which made Siri scream at him as never before: "Put that right back! Or I'll go away forever!"

During this period Johannes became my truest companion and confidant. I had the feeling that he was the only one who could still understand me, even though he existed only in an engraving. I'd found his picture in one of my twin books and cut it out. It fit into the beautiful old wooden frame that I'd once bought with Iris for the "Iris-Madonna with Siri" photo. Johannes hung just high enough over the foot of my bed that I could see him as I lay there comfortably and carried on a conversation with him.

Johannes was the asymmetrical, attached twin of Lazarus Coloredo. The brothers lived in Genoa in the seventeenth century. Lazarus, who'd grown to normal size, bore Johannes, the small twin, on his breast. Johannes's head and torso hung slackly toward the back and his mouth was open. He seemed to be sleeping—at least, his eyes were always closed. His arms and legs dangled like the limbs of a rag doll.

This half-human was a parasite. He didn't eat, but he nourished himself on the larger twin and let his brother supply him with blood. Lazarus, on the other hand, was what is called an "autosite" in scientific terminology, one who does not need the other and controls him. Johannes was only a patient hanger-on.

No book that told Johannes's story ever answered the questions I wanted to ask him:

—Did you ever open your eyes and look him in the face?
—Did you ever talk with each other?
—Didn't you want to see the world, or were you blind?
—Could you influence him with your own thoughts?
—Did you love each other or hate each other?

—Did you have your own feelings, or did you only feel
through him and everything he felt?
—Were you as feelingless as me?

But Johannes remained dumb. He couldn't give me the
answers I was seeking. No person knew the answer, not even
centuries later in the era of the cloned parasite. I knew just
one thing for sure: The Sellin twins had no more future.
The black hole of the present was growing larger and was
swallowing us. I couldn't get free of Iris either. My life clung
to hers the way Johannes's life had depended on Lazarus.

When Iris Sellin slowly turned from a famous composer
into a person in need of care, the public was at first
interested in her plight. Everyone regretted that she could
no longer compose, and they mourned the great loss for
modern music. Sympathy for her was accompanied by a
mixture of pity and sensationalism. Sales of her CDs
increased greatly. On the occasion of her fiftieth birthday,
the "outstanding representative of the new classical music"
was even rediscovered. Her music was heard more often in
concert halls, and countless articles appeared about her.

Siri read them all and marveled. Many women revered
her mother as a cult figure, and they celebrated her not only
as a composer but also as a courageous pioneer of "modern
virgin conception" and of "biological self-realization." A few
had asked what was happening with the clone daughter.
Wasn't she following in her mother's footsteps?

Iris no longer gave interviews, so they came to me: journalists, music students, admirers of Iris's music. All of them wanted to hear something personal from me about her and our relationship. I refused all their inquiries, because I couldn't yet talk about her/me/us. My own life was slipping away from me.

I was eighteen, and in my fantasies I was once again playing the Iyou game with you, Iris. But our text had changed:

"You'll look just like me someday, when you're big. And then you'll be the sick one," you said.

"I'm going to be even uglier and sicker!" I cried proudly. And then I asked anxiously, "Will you already be dead then?"

"Of course!" said Iris, with a laugh.

"I don't want you to die, ever!" I cried.

You hugged me and said, "Because there is you, we'll die together. Then I am you and you are I." I shook with fear.

By the time I finally passed my school-leaving exams at nineteen, I had no strength left. Wearily I dragged myself to courses at the art academy that Janeck had found for me to at least give my life a temporary structure. But in the fall I packed away all my pictures, brushes, and paints.

In the two last years of her double life, Siri often stood in front of the mirror and made herself up slowly and carefully. But what she was saying when her lips moved while she did it, Janeck never found out. She had given up coloring her hair, and she no longer wore explosively colorful clothes but went back to black and gray, like Iris.

When Janeck asked her why she wore those boring things, Siri stood very stiff, with twitching eyebrows. "How can anyone change her spots," she said, "when they aren't even her own spots?"

She kept comparing her mirror image with photographs of Iris when she'd been nineteen and twenty like her. Sometimes she played Iris, like that time at the hospital when she'd fooled old Oma Katharina. Shortly after the commotion about the composer's fiftieth birthday, Siri had gone into a music store and given out autographs as Iris Sellin. No one unmasked the doppelgänger, but she no longer found any pleasure in that. The time for jokes was past.

Siri was a boundary walker: She balanced on the border that ran between the two lives, and sometimes she lost her balance and fell off, either into the life of her mother or into a dark nothingness.

Only rarely did my rage blaze up, and so when it did, it was all the more destructive and wild. Then, Iris, your misbreed felt fouled and filthied, misused and maltreated. I would remember how I'd grabbed the fruit knife and threatened you. And again I'd hear the metallic clink of the knife on the floor.

I stood alone before the mirror, and I drew the point of the scissors along my left arm, from the hand to the shoulder. When I felt the cold metal on my throat, I got gooseflesh. Then the blade moved toward the place where my/your/our heart thumped. One jab, and that would be the end of the storybook twins. I giggled at my joke, as the sharp edge tickled my neck.

In the twenty-first year, Professor Fisher came to a medical congress in Hamburg. He'd announced his visit to Iris, but she didn't want to see him. When Fisher asked about Siri, Daniela Hausmann gave him Janeck's telephone number.

After Fisher's message that he would like to invite Janeck and Siri to dinner, Janeck immediately called him at his hotel. "I'll try to persuade Siri," he promised the doctor. He earnestly hoped that meeting with Fisher could call forth something in his little sister that would drive away her despair. He didn't conceal from Fisher how matters stood with Iris's daughter.

"Of course I'll come too," he promised Siri when she agreed almost indifferently to the meeting.

Not far from Janeck's apartment there was an Italian bistro that wasn't too chic or too noisy. The three stood there facing each other somewhat stiffly at first, but then Professor Fisher said to Siri, "I just wanted to see you. So you decide this evening where we sit, what we eat, and what we talk about."

They talked about all kinds of things—about school and books, the latest films, Fisher's meetings—but never about Iris. Siri chose a pasta dish for each of them and the appropriate red wine. She became more and more lively as the wine went to her head a bit, and Janeck was relieved. He gave Siri a kiss on the cheek because it was such a marvelous "Siri-thaw evening." Fisher joined the laughter and placed his hand on Siri's arm.

Suddenly Siri became serious. "You have beautiful hands, such slender fingers, Professor!" she said. "I have often dreamed of your hands, since I met you the first time. Do you remember our first meeting?" Fisher nodded.

"Just eleven—no, ten, I was," she continued, "and I practiced so terribly much, because I wanted to be a pianist like Iris, only better." Siri took his right hand and placed it against her cheek, and it almost sounded as though she were singing a children's song: "My father, my father has such beautiful hands, has such beautiful hands...." Uncomfortable and helpless, Fisher looked over at Janeck.

When Siri felt his withdrawal, she only held his hand more firmly. "You are a kind of father for me—or aren't you?" Her voice became aggressive. "Is it distasteful to you to touch me? Don't you like the feeling of your creation? Do I make you nervous?" Then she was very gentle again. "Dear Papa," she almost whispered. "You with your beautiful hands! Where were you when I was missing you? I so often missed a father in those days, although Iris tried to be everything."

Fisher grew calmer. "Iris is a very exceptional woman," he said.

"Be quiet!" Siri let go of his hand and pushed Fisher's shoulder so hard that he almost fell off his chair.

Janeck stood up and took hold of Siri firmly. "Calm down. He doesn't mean any harm." And with a slight movement of his head, Janne indicated to Fisher that it would probably be better if he left.

"It's late, after eleven already. I'd like to go home," Janeck said to Siri.

Fisher nodded almost imperceptibly and moved slowly away.

"Filthy, filthy! They stink. Those beautiful hands are damned filthy." Siri voice was staccato and grew louder and louder. "You have dirtied your beautiful doctor's hands. Dirty, dirty . . . are you going to wash your hands now?"

Fisher stopped at the bar and handed his credit card to the cashier.

"To divide someone in two means to kill him. Didn't you know that, Professor?" Siri was now screaming through the entire restaurant, so that Fisher, and all the other patrons, had to hear it.

Fisher murmured an apology and left the restaurant with a beet-red face.

Today I understand what Fisher had wanted: to talk about Iris so that I would know and understand and ultimately forgive him and her. Maybe soon I'll be able to talk with him, if he has read my writings. I'm ashamed when I think back to that evening. But at that time I was no longer entirely of this world—I was going crazy in my double life.

Iris altered at fast-forward speed. At fifty-one she looked like a woman in her middle sixties. I observed her every new wrinkle and liver spot, the thinning hair and knotty fingers, and I looked at myself, seeing how I slowly faded. Still, life chained us together. But more and more often I longed for death—whether it was her death or my own didn't matter.

Or was I wishing that both of us were in the grave?

By the spring of the twenty-first year, Iris and Siri had developed a firm visiting ritual. Iris no longer had to beg her daughter to come, and Siri never had to refuse—now, every two weeks, Siri went to Lübeck on Tuesday afternoons. At about five o'clock she entered the old apartment, where Dada awaited her and told her the latest over a cup of coffee. Then the visitor went into the workroom where now, instead of the long wooden table with the crackling parchment sheets, there was a hospital bed. From there Iris could look out of the bay window at the old trees in front of the house.

On some days Iris was as determined and demanding as she used to be. "Why don't you play anymore?" she would ask. "As talented as you are! You'll regret it yet. You'll never make up for what you're missing now. And what else are you going to do with your life?"

"I don't know yet," Siri would answer, "I'm just a good-for-nothing."

On other days Iris didn't say a word. She lay still, with glassy eyes, doubled up under the covers, every fiber of her body aching. Siri felt then how her mother suffered. In this mood they sometimes grew very close, and they were in unison again. When Iris looked at her daughter and saw the young Iris, she was comforted: Yes, she would live on, everything was all right. And a feeling of peace came over her.

Often, too, the visits were unbearable. Iris sometimes carped at and abused Siri, who didn't come often enough, and lived with that Janeck in Hamburg, and furthermore was living on her money and was only ungrateful.

It was in the fall that Iris did not recognize her daughter
for the first time. She stared in panic at the door through
which this stranger was entering. With difficulty, she pulled
herself up by the steel triangle that dangled from the frame
over her hospital bed and screeched, "Who are you? How
did you get in here?" The person approached menacingly,
and Iris screamed for help.

Actually, Siri was intending to take her in her arms and
say, "It's just me, Siri, your daughter."

But her mother hissed at her, "Get out of here! Out!"
And then she screamed for Daniela Hausmann, "Where are
you, Dada, for heaven's sake. . . . "

Siri backed out of the room and collided in the hallway
with Dada, who comforted her and cuddled her as she had
when Siri was a child. These days it happened more and
more often that Iris didn't recognize someone and was
confused and aggressive.

The day that Iris didn't recognize me for the first time, I
forgot to go into the music room and say hello to Mr. Black.
I ran past the tall hall mirror and kept hearing Iris screaming. I just wanted to go home. There was nothing more for
me here. It was as if I were dead. I ran outside and breathed
in the clear fall air. Leaves were falling from the trees, and
the late beams of the autumn sun deepened their reds and
golds. Their damp upper surfaces glittered after the morning
rain. A short train ride, and finally I was lying on my bed
and with Johannes again, who had been waiting for me.

"You know me, but she didn't know me today," I told him. "Maybe I should have said, my name is Johanna. Because I'm like you. I know that creepy-nice feeling of not being able to do anything, of always being carried, motionless. Did you both die at the same time?" I asked my companions in suffering. "It's probably not even a scary feeling at all when you die. A big rest. No more fighting, and finally no more questions."

The past and present were dissolving. Iris hadn't recognized me, so there was no me anymore. And as I talked with Johannes, I was floating up high into a timeless space.

Iris Sellin's condition continued to worsen. At the beginning of December she was admitted to the hospital with pneumonia, and she never left it again.

It was January of the twenty-second year, and the first snow was finally falling. "How long does she have to live?" Siri asked the doctor. No one dies of MS, he explained to her, but they die of the after-effects, infections. It could go on this way for another four weeks, or for many months. Very probably her mother would not survive the year.

The doctor showed Siri the CT scan of her mother's brain. It was riddled with white spots. Not only was her body shriveled, but her intellect and her personality lay dying. This view inside Iris's head allowed Siri to understand better what made her so paralyzed and helpless: Her feelings had no opposite anymore. She could no longer despise or pity this mother, and so she hated herself that much more.

I had the feeling that those white spots were spreading in my head too. Iris had not recognized me and I no longer recognized Iris. Again we resembled each other—one brain like the other, one heart and one soul.

In the Middle Ages theologians argued vigorously about what happened to the inseparable souls of twins after death if one had been a bad person and the other a good one. Did the souls of both burn in hellfire, or did they sing together in heaven? Or, were they separated for eternity?

I asked Johannes: How does one twin prepare for the death of the other? How does a clone child prepare for the death of the clone mother? What comes next? Will I too become ill? Is everything predetermined genetically? Am I not just twenty-one years old, but also thirty years older, just like her?

It's not only skin and bones that are grown together, or organs that must be divided into two people, that make for inseparability. Feelings too—especially clone feelings— bind two people together, until death separates them.

Must I really die with her? I asked Johannes over and over again. But my confidant kept his silence.

How long Siri stayed with the patient ceased to matter. If she were only with her a short time, it could be that Iris would thank her for the long visit. If she sat beside the bed for an hour, Iris would reproach her the next week for not coming for months.

Iris Sellin was already living outside of normal earth time. She fussed about the yellow ribbon that Siri had donned secretly for the Mother's Day concert. She screamed for Taiwo and Kehinde and demanded manuscript paper and ink.

"She often calls for her sister," the nurse said to Siri one day. "We had no idea she had a sister. Couldn't she come sometimes?"

"She's having delusions. She doesn't have a sister anymore," Siri answered.

She saw the open sores on Iris's back when the nurse turned her on her side to change the bedding. And it seemed to Siri that she was looking at her own body. She shivered.

It was so cold in the room. "Scalpel!" cried the pathologist, and he urged his assistant to proceed carefully. He had never before had such clones under the knife. Never under the glittering, bluish neon light had he been so close to the secret of age. He wanted to work layer by layer, to take their innermost cores apart and compare them down to the last cell nuclei.

"How long till June?" asked a voice.

They couldn't keep me here that long, thought Siri. Not in this cold, all cut up, on this hateful metal table.

"How long till June?" But she knew the voice. It belonged to Iris. And Siri realized she was not lying on a hard dissecting table. She was sitting on a chair next to the sickbed. The wind had opened the window sash, and that was why she was shivering.

"How long till June?" Iris's impatient voice sounded again.

Now I knew when you would die. You intended to fight death until the zodiac sign of Gemini, the twins—of which Castor and Pollux are the principal stars—appeared in the heavens. You would not give up until then. You were composing your own death, Iris, not leaving anything to chance, even at the bitter end! Finding the suitable point in time for your disappearance.

And when I said to you, "It's already spring. We're at the beginning of May," you answered, "A lovely time to be pregnant."

You turned back to the beginning of our life together. "The Anna Perenna music follows a bell shape. Don't you hear the bells? Ding, dong, ding! Ding, dong, ding!" you sang with the voice of a small girl. Then your eyes closed.

Once again you started up. "Do you have my diaries?" you asked, and suddenly you seemed very clear. "They're all for you, don't forget! It's my legacy. I've written everything down for you."

And as you fell asleep I listened to you softly murmuring, "How long till June?" I swore to myself never to read those books.

In the first warm early summer night, at the end of May, Janeck heard his little sister scream and ran into her room. Siri was sitting up in her bed, bathed in sweat.

"It was only a dream," she said, and she told Janeck falteringly of the parasite that had weighed down her chest. "I had no idea how heavy such a deadweight could be. He had his head turned to the side and he let his arms and legs dangle. When I tried to lift the head to pat the dry lips with a damp cloth, I looked into the face of my mother. She opened her eyes and she was surprised and frightened and said, "Who are you? Go away!" I shook the torso, though it was growing out of me, until finally it fell away. That's probably when I screamed. I was expecting a horrible pain and was afraid I was bleeding. But nothing hurt, and there was no blood either, no wound, only a big, dark hole and . . . and . . . " Siri looked for a word, " . . . lightness. But I screamed again anyway, and then I woke up."

Janeck lay down beside Siri and held her hand until she fell asleep again and was breathing quietly.

The next day Siri thought about this dream without fear. She was certain now that everything would be over soon. And finally Janeck might take down the picture of Johannes and tear it to pieces.

The nurses in the hospital told Siri at her next visit that her mother had had a terrible nightmare two days before. She had sat up in bed, bathed in sweat, and had screamed terribly. It was the same night when Siri had torn out the parasite in her dream.

Iris didn't notice Siri when she walked into the room. She lay quietly and seemed to be thinking about something lovely. Siri hummed some of the melodies that her mother had sung her to sleep with when she was a little girl. Life seemed to be running backwards.

The call from the nurse came on June 13 of the twenty-second year. "She asked for you," said the voice. "I think the end is coming. If you want to be here, you'd better hurry."

Siri took the next train. This time the ram-ta-ta, ram-ta-ta of the wheels did not calm her. Before she got to Lübeck, she counted the seven towers in the distance and marveled that they were all still standing. When Iris dies, she thought, the entire world is going to collapse and turn to dust like my wish notes in the old roof vaulting.

All the windows were open and a summer breeze wafted through the hospital room. Siri held the hand of the dying woman. Once during her death struggle Iris opened her eyes and a smile of recognition flitted over her face.

I'm sorry I didn't play well enough, Iris. And so you must die.

How thin your fingers are, as slender as Fisher's fingers. Only death will fulfill my wish to have long, slender pianist's hands. But I don't need them anymore.

A gray veil moved up over your face from below, Motwi, and an incredible silence enveloped us. It must have been the same silence in which Mortimer Gabriel Fisher watched the Iris clone begin to live under his telemicroscope. At the beginning and end of life is peace.

A circle closed.

Siri gazed into the face of the corpse and found in it the little child and the girl they both had been. And she saw in it the old woman she would be one day. But the young woman who had sat by the deathbed as Iris drew her last breath suddenly vanished.

Siri looked for her desperately.

She bent over the dead woman as if over a mirror, and she felt her own eyebrows and those of the body. Her index finger slid along the two nose bridges. She felt the curve of two pairs of lips and of the two similar chins. Siri had to comprehend and feel all over again where the other one stopped and she herself began. Who was dead and who was still living?

Someone sighed. The sigh had come from Siri's mouth. Now she felt that she was in fact still breathing, was still alive. But Iris did not move; she remained deathly still.

Finally tears came to Siri's eyes and she could cry. She wept because she was sad, and she wept out of fear of having to live alone. Iris had left her clone doubly alone, as daughter and as twin. But Siri also wept for joy, to be allowed to live alone at last.

For the first time in my life I could look at you without asking myself what you wanted from me.

Almost twenty-two years after my birth, on a June summer day, I could for the first time say *I* without lying. I had become an I, unique and for the first time undivided, finally an individual.

I looked into your still face, pale sister, and was more certain of myself than ever before: That you are you alone and not I. Suddenly everything was so clear, dead Mother, so easy and simple. I was living and you were dead. Two people could not be any more different than we were at this moment.

And when I felt that and had grasped it, our/my/your life ceased to be a double life. On that day, my second year zero began.

Siri even dared to go back to the island of the twins, for now there was room. "Hello, Mr. Black! Long time no see," she murmured as she stroked the gleaming instrument. And because she was lonely, she lay down under the black wooden body as she used to do. And she cried until she had no tears left.

When Siri crawled out from under the instrument, she was utterly calm. She opened the cover of the concert piano, plucked the strings, looked at the hammers, pressed the keys. Then she sat down on the piano stool. Her hands wanted to play again.

In all the years I hadn't played, I'd forgotten astonishingly little. I suppose it was because I'd played so often in my dreams. My fingers found the right keys without effort. I mixed *Dewdrops* with *Echoes*, improvised in major and minor. But I would still have to practice much more to not disgrace you this time. My very last performance was going to be at your funeral. Doggedly I worked on the funeral dirge for you, Iris, that was also going to be my new cradlesong.

The flower-covered coffin stood on a dais. When Siri made her entrance at the end of the funeral, a trap door in the floor would open, and Iris would disappear forever.

Many people had come, and when Siri took her place in the first row with Dada and Janeck, she heard a voice behind her whisper, "Wow, what a resemblance! You'd think it was Iris. Absolutely creepy!"

Siri paid no attention to these words or to the many speeches that were given. She didn't remember even one of the eulogies later, either. She was thinking only of her performance.

"As a song of farewell, you will now hear an improvisation, played by Siri Sellin." A brief murmur ran through the funeral hall when Thomas Weber announced the daughter. Slowly Siri walked over to the piano, feeling those avid singleton-looks on her back. But they couldn't harm her anymore. Iris would never upstage her again. Iris was dead, and Siri was one of a kind. This knowledge was with her when she started to play.

When I began to play, I forgot everything around me. I played only for you, Mother, just as you had played for me when I was still living in the dark inside you and was invisible to others.

My beginning was your end; your end is my beginning.

Not only did I play for the prearranged ten minutes, but I kept on playing, even after the coffin had disappeared. I entrapped the listeners in my spell the way I had dreamed before my first solo concert. With the last chord still floating through the room, a man leaped up, clapping, and cried "Bravo!" He had completely forgotten where he was. Then everyone stood up and applauded me.

You had to die first, Iris, so that I got to hear the applause I was entitled to and was meant for me alone.

Siri stood beside Thomas Weber at the exit of the funeral chapel. She shook many hands, thanked others for their expressions of sympathy, and longed the whole time to be at the shore.

This evening I'd like to run along the beach with Janeck, she thought to herself, with bare feet and the wind in my face. I'd like to taste the salt on my lips and throw myself on the warm sand. I want to lie on my back and look up into the dark blue of the sky.

Most of the faces that passed by her were unimportant shadows. But then she found herself looking into a pair of eyes that she would never forget. They belonged to Kristian, her first great love. Siri looked at Kristian and imagined that he would embrace her and whisper in her ear that he absolutely wanted to meet her, now that Iris, who had so long stood between them, was dead. He'd thought only about Siri over the years and could never forget her. Siri felt herself blushing.

But Kristian only put his hands on her shoulders and gave her a gentle kiss on the forehead. "You are very brave," he said. "Iris would have been proud of you, and especially of your playing." His eyes were wet with tears.

He's still too cowardly to say what he wants to me, Siri

thought. Wordlessly she turned her face to the next mourner. Kristian took his hands from her shoulders and moved on without saying anything more. Siri did not look after him, or she would have seen him pause for a moment before he finally left.

Suddenly the last one in the long line of mourners stretched toward her two hands that she recalled very well. Mortimer G. Fisher had come to the funeral. And once again this man to whom she owed her life was standing before her. She thought of their last meeting and was uncertain what she should say or do now. But Fisher grasped her hands, as all the others had done too.

"There's one question I have always wanted to ask you," said Siri. "Did you actually make love to my mother?"

"No, there was never that possibility." Mortimer Fisher looked sad. This young woman who so very much resembled her mother made him painfully aware of how old he was getting. And he sensed how terrible it must have been for Iris to constantly encounter her youthful image.

"You must play again," he said. "Promise me that, Siri? You really are as gifted as your mother."

What did Fisher really want from me? He was interfering again, still giving me advice after Iris's death! He had no right to do that anymore. And so I defended myself, as helpless as a little girl who was held fast and could not move. I pulled my hands away and spat at him.

When I saw my spittle on Fisher's jacket, I was ashamed. I was twenty-two years old and no longer a child, but in Fisher's presence I always felt so small and helpless, and at the same time a terrible rage rose in me. Luckily the rest of the mourners hadn't noticed what had happened.

Fisher remained very calm—no exclamation, no movement, nothing. He even stroked my hair almost tenderly. "Please don't apologize," he said. "I only hope that we'll meet again under the right circumstances, to finally talk in peace, little Siri. It would do us both good, I believe."

My rebellious rage seemed especially childish to me now. "I'll consider it," was all I answered.

We left in different directions. Janeck was waiting for me, and we drove to the seashore where once again I joined in the screaming lamentation of the gulls.

Two days after the funeral Siri Sellin received a letter from the New Classics recording company, which had formerly recorded her mother's concerts. After the director-manager Roger Wimmer had offered her his condolences and apologized for his haste, he made Siri an offer. He'd heard she was playing again, and he would gladly organize a concert tour for her. He asked her to call him to discuss everything further on the phone.

Siri carried the letter around with her for two days before she called.

The manager came to the phone immediately. "New Classics, Wimmer speaking."

"This is Iris Sellin," said Siri.

"I beg your pardon. . . ?" Wimmer sounded at a loss.

"It's supposed to be a joke. This is her daughter, Siri

Sellin. You wrote me."

Wimmer's restrained laugh showed that he didn't quite know how he should handle this situation. "I must say—the similarity of the voices—incredible! You really threw me."

And then he explained that from the commercial point of view it would certainly be advisable to move as quickly as possible. The name Sellin was on everyone's lips at the moment—because of a sad occurrence, to be sure, but it could still be used as a draw—

"I understand you very clearly, I think," Siri interrupted him. "You intend for me to get myself up as Iris Sellin. Title of the first part of the concert, 'Music from the Grave.' And then, after the intermission, I'm Siri Sellin and play as the daughter under the title, 'Risen from the Dead' or—let me think—'As a Newborn' would probably be even better."

Siri's irony unsettled Wimmer even further. He swallowed audibly. "I hadn't actually thought so specifically. . . . "

An embarrassed silence followed, then Wimmer went on. "Somewhat daring, your idea, but not uninteresting. It's not bad, but I'd need to think about it some more."

Siri could hardly grasp it: This person actually had found her suggestion worth considering. Was everyone crazy except her, or was it the other way around?

"Do you know the line my mother especially loved to quote?" Siri asked. "No? Swine and composers have one thing in common: They're both worth the most when they're dead."

Roger Wimmer laughed much too loud. He had no idea what to think of this woman and her macabre wit. "I'll get back to you in the next few days."

Siri briefly said good-bye and hung up. She went
directly to the chest of drawers in the hall. The big scissors
were still in the second drawer on the right, and she slowly
drew them out from under a scarf.

I could appear again . . . swish onto the stage like Iris, surrounded by applause . . . a tour with sold-out concert
halls . . . I'd show them all . . . my wish note has brought me
luck . . . I want to become a great pianist . . . I'll make you
healthy with my music . . . I will let Iris rise again . . . in the
name of the mother and the daughter and the holy gene-
ghost . . . because there is you, I will never die . . . clone
duty fulfilled . . . I'm playing for my life . . . I stand on the
stage . . . everyone cheers me . . . the beautiful blue dress
must still be in the closet . . . there's the blueprint dress
. . . does it still fit me? . . . I slip into it . . . you are my
life . . . quick to the mirror . . . from all angles, the dress fits
as if I were poured into it . . . I spin in a circle . . . Siri-Iris-
Iris-Siri . . . Do you see two or four eyes? . . . Only two! . . . I
will become a pianist when I'm big . . . YouI thinks the dress
is too long . . . I will be bigger and more famous . . . wait,
Iyou takes the big fabric shears . . . are you already dead,
then? . . . we'll just cut some off . . . *rip, snip,* DNA. *Rip,
snip,* DNA . . . because there is you, I will never die
. . . careful, it's crooked . . . another piece has to come off
. . . but the scissors slipped . . . you shouldn't cut up the
dress! . . . you'll cut yourself, YouI . . . already did . . . only a
little scratch, Iyou . . . *rip, snip,* DNA . . . blood makes spots
. . . the dress is ruined anyhow . . . don't cry . . . now I can't

perform . . . that's nothing to cry about. . . but I don't have a dress to wear . . . you're really bleeding . . . I'll cancel tomorrow . . . the dress is ruined.

Daniela Hausmann was terribly frightened when she saw Siri lying on the floor in a cut-up dress. Bloody scratches marked her bare legs and arms, and the bloody scissors lay beside her. She knelt down beside Siri and looked into a smiling face. Siri had not looked so at peace for a very long time.

"I'm all right, Dada," said Siri, "really. It's behind me."

Piles of boxes were sitting ready for collection in the Sellin apartment. The cartons in the workroom were to go to the archives and the library of the Academy of Music. They contained the piano practice program that Iris had developed for her daughter, the unfinished sketches and the finished compositions exclusive of the two opera scores, collected notes, and her CD collection.

Four specially marked boxes held Iris's photo albums and diaries. Some she had begun as a teenager, while other volumes came from her student days. Starting in the year zero and continuing into the twentieth year, Iris had kept a diary regularly and painstakingly tracked every detail of Siri's development and musical progress. Daniela Hausmann had read the black notebooks and told Siri about them, but Siri refused to even take the books in her hand.

Siri had not known of the diaries until her mother had spoken of them a few weeks before her death, calling them "my legacy." Iris had been writing secretly all those years and no one had been aware of it. But Siri did not want to know how she would feel at age twenty-five or thirty or forty. Or how Iris had viewed her clone. She'd already written about that herself. Her own record, which she was calling *Blueprint*, was almost finished.

After Janeck had driven Siri to the trash recycling center and they had dumped all the diaries into the gigantic paper shredder, they drove back to Hamburg. Then Siri sent five pictures she had painted, along with the necessary application papers, to the Academy of Art in Berlin. Neither Siri nor Janeck had any doubt that she would be accepted. In her twenty-third year Siri was going to begin her art studies.

"I'm stronger than the others," Siri said to him, "because I've survived my own death."

She had no money worries. The royalties from Iris's compositions made her entirely free to do or not do whatever she wanted. Painting would only be the beginning. Siri had a boundless eagerness to try new things and to find new forms. Everything should become different, bolder, more radical. What would her art be like, then? Janeck asked.

"Simply cloney," was Siri's answer.

I have brought only two things from the long-lost island of the twins with me into my single life: the white marble statue of the double goddess, and our black concert grand piano, at which I have written all this. Mr. Black is always supposed to remind me that I am a surviving twin. The piano is my *ibeji*.

Ibeji is what the African Yoruba call the small figure that a woodcutter makes after the death of a twin. The soul of the dead twin dwells in this carving. This wooden figure accompanies the survivor into his new life so that he is not left half a person. For the Africans believe that the soul of twins is indivisible, even after death.

First ending, in July
of the twenty-second year

Pollux Seul
Ten Years Later

I am now thirty-one years old. Just as old as Iris was in the year zero when she conceived me. And like Iris, I also live alone and only for my art. I have managed to become just as famous as Iris was at that time—not because I am her blueprint, but because I finally could become I. I hardly ever speak of clonehood anymore; it has become a very commonplace form of parenthood now. I am no longer anything unusual in this respect, and so no one at the opening of my first major show ever asked about "the mother of the artist."

My first one-woman show in Hamburg, which just closed, was a gigantic success, and I am very proud of that. On my own, I count, and especially with my artist pseudonym *Double-Blue*. Everyone who knows me understands the meaning of it, and among those are you, dear *Blueprint* reader. Janeck had a good laugh over my wordplay.

But I will not tolerate any joking about my artist's biography. Although it's often smiled at or dismissed as egocentric, I insist that my biography not begin with my actual birth year but with the year of Iris's death, which I

call my second year zero. That is the year in which I wrote
Blueprint.

What has happened to me and in me since then can be
seen and understood in my art alone. Nothing else is
anybody's business. Some critics described the works in my
Hamburg show as "very sensitive and yet extreme;" others
described them as "calculated but still full of emotion."
These were almost the same words that greeted Iris's first
successful compositions, in fact. Thomas Weber brought me
some of her old concert reviews a few days after the
preview. He'd underlined the repeated phrases with a red
pen—not blue, fortunately! What did I think of the
parallels, he wanted to know.

Double-Blue just shrugged her shoulders coolly. "It
doesn't shock me and it doesn't please me," I said. "But it
doesn't surprise me anymore, either. I've known for a long
time that Siri is becoming like Iris."

Often in my sculptures, which are driven to move by
small electric motors, hard and soft materials are
juxtaposed, creating a sense of almost unbearable tension
and menace. Metal fans open to display feathers and paper,
or sometimes old letters. Knives attack brushes or wooden
laths. Water and paints drip onto iron frames. Sharp,
pointed metal targets eggs.

"An entirely new kind of machine art is being born
here," said Katinka Frischmut, the owner of the Hamburg
Galerie Local Time, at the opening. She paused dramatically
for a moment before she continued. "Machines play a major
role in Siri Sellin's installations. Are these metal construc-
tions that seemingly live forever? Do these constructed

aliens perhaps substitute for or symbolize eternal life?"

I have always rejected any such point of view, making clear that there are no eternal machines. Like us humans, they have only a limited life span. And so the machines I construct are by no means perfect either. They quiver and tremble, they faint and suddenly awaken to new life again. They dance and make noises, they become independent or go crazy, or at least pretend to. They act as if they were alive, and they live in a world entirely their own. They perform like actors on a stage and so they hold a mirror up to us. For in this world we are all melancholy actors in utter solitariness.

While the audience was applauding the gallery owner, an attractive man came up to me and smiled at me as if I were an old acquaintance. I combed my memory and then gave a start. A piece of my past was suddenly standing there before me in the flesh. I'd even been on the lookout for him, but the man I'd invited and been expecting would have had to be much older looking.

Quickly I counted back: He must be exactly sixty-eight years old. We'd last met four years after Iris's funeral, and he'd told me a lot of important things then. But the man in front of me was only a few years older than I was.

Before I could say anything, the man introduced himself in English: "Hello, I'm Jonathan Fisher, Professor Fisher's son. You've probably guessed that already—my father and I also look very much alike."

He had actually said "also," and I was annoyed at this singleton I didn't know who, like you, knew or understood nothing about real likeness.

"I'm very happy to meet you." Fisher's voice indicated that he really meant it.

He studied me attentively and appeared to like what he saw. He saw what his father had seen a long time ago: grayish blue eyes in a slightly rounded face, which looked stern and created distance. Hair that fell over a high forehead and stood up somewhat tousled and unruly on my head. Nicely curving lips, but rather narrow, and when they weren't laughing, they looked somewhat wry. A winning smile, though its effect is probably somewhat arrogant.

"My father has told me so much about you," Fisher continued. "He was delighted to get your invitation. So he was very sad that he couldn't come himself, but he suffered a stroke six months ago that left him paralyzed on one side. Only slightly, fortunately, but it's slowed him down so much that this long trip would have been too much for him. And so he sent me as his stand-in. It was very important to him. And believe me, I'm standing in for him very gladly, really very gladly."

I liked Jonathan Fisher. We stood face to face as his father and my mother had stood face to face a long time ago. And then this son put his hand on my arm. Perhaps Professor Mortimer G. Fisher had touched Iris Sellin the same way. I seemed to have fallen into an old film.

Startled, I closed my eyes. Suddenly the only thing that existed for me was this touch; I felt only his hand. Then in my belly something contracted. It was a feeling that I knew only too well: I was a child again, looking through the hole in the gloomy gallery, deep down into the nave of the church. And I was a teenager gazing infatuatedly at Kristian.

At that moment I would have liked to whisper tenderly in Jonathan Fisher's ear, "Love me on the spot. Let's make a child." Why did this dumb, impossible, old-fashioned thought suddenly come to me, and moreover with this stranger whom I scarcely knew? I was shocked. I had never realized I could even think such a thing. Too often I'd sworn face to face with YouI and Iyou never to clone a child or conceive one with a man. No children! That was definite! I would never waver—and now this.

"Never," whispered Double-Blue.

"Sorry, I didn't understand you. Aren't you feeling well? You're trembling!" Jonathan Fisher sounded concerned and grasped my arm again.

I shook my head, blinked my eyes, and smiled back carefully. "It's nothing. I was just thinking of something."

Relieved, Fisher let go of me and talked on. "My father has been in touch with an art gallery."

Why doesn't someone turn the sound off? I asked myself. The film has been over for a long time now and the lead actors are gone. Why doesn't he stop talking? Why doesn't he just go away? Our roles are fulfilled; the game is over.

Fisher's voice seemed to be far away, but I understood exactly what he was saying. "There's a tremendous amount of interest in your work. Perhaps you'll come to Canada and visit us soon."

We were both silent then while around us the guests chattered and laughed. A curious tension was rebuilding between us. I looked at the hand that was again lying on my arm. I saw the wedding ring on Fisher's ring finger, and I noticed he had the same beautiful, slender hands as his father.

I shook off his hand with a very determined movement of my arm, looking him in the face as I did so. He must have found that provocative and seductive, for he gave me a challenging look. And so he was hurt by how hard and cold my voice sounded when I said to him, "I hate duplications, Mr. Fisher. And I'm afraid of old stories, especially reruns. You can certainly understand that. It's no accident that this show is taking place just now. When I was twenty-nine and then thirty years old, I had a horrible and—probably for you—unimaginable terror. I was afraid of becoming ill, ill like my mother when she was exactly the same age as me. This grisly fear ruled my life. It halted time. I no longer had a future. But now that too is over and done with."

After a short silence I said, "I don't know what I would have done if I had become ill, if I'd gotten MS. Maybe I would have first killed your father and then myself. Don't look so shocked! It's because I wanted to say precisely that to your father that I invited him, that false angel Gabriel."

The last words had sounded hateful, and clearly Jonathan Fisher was asking himself if I really had said "angel." He grabbed my hand, perhaps because he sensed how tense I was, and probably also because he just wanted to touch me once more. And for a very brief moment I enjoyed his touch again. But I was immediately ashamed of this new weakness and grabbed my hand back even more vigorously, so that his wedding ring scraped the skin on the back of my hand. The short, sharp pain finally freed me entirely.

Fisher must not have any more opportunities to get too close to me. Therefore Double-Blue suggested, "Let me take you through the show so that you have something to report when you get back home."

Where my work was concerned, I was in a world of my own. There I felt safe, safe even from him.

As we came to the end of the circuit, we were standing under the big central installation of the show. This piece had been especially well received by the public and the critics. It was entitled "Pollux Seul," and it consisted of a black grand piano that hung upside down from the ceiling on thick steel cables.

Jonathan Fisher looked up at it apprehensively. The gleaming monster, its legs touching the ceiling, appeared about to fall any moment and crush all who looked at it from below. But the longer you looked, the more this fear diminished. After a time, you saw only a helpless thing up there. I could tell by Fisher's facial expression, which slowly relaxed, that the piece affected him in this way.

At times—not at precise intervals, but irregularly and unexpectedly—this instrument vomited its white keys and then its black, the twins and triplets, and its little hammers. The clattering and groaning that fell from the wooden body was only frightening the first time; afterwards the retching was almost funny, even ridiculous. Then with deep groans, the metal strings and wooden viscera were withdrawn into the innards of the music machine, and the black concert grand again hung solitary and still on the ceiling, as if nothing had happened. But soon afterward the tormented instrument heaved and vomited again.

I know what you're thinking, dear *Blueprint* readers, but it's wrong. The concert piano on the gallery ceiling was not

Mr. Black. He has been sitting in my apartment for ten years, unplayed. Of course I've dusted him now and again.

Why did I give this work the name "Pollux Seul," Jonathan Fisher wanted to know. I'd already been asked that a number of times, and I'd always answered with the following story:

"Castor and Pollux were the twin sons of Leda and Zeus. In the form of a swan, under the peaks of the Taygetus, he sired these children, which hatched from a swan's egg. The brothers ruled the winds and the waves, and sailors made them into their patrons. When Castor— this twin was mortal—fell in battle, he went down to Hades. On the other hand, Zeus took the immortal Pollux up to the gods on Olympus. But the two brothers did not want to be separated. So they agreed to pass their days together, one day in the underworld, one day on Olympus. That, at least, is what the legends say about these inseparables who were separated.

"The principal stars in the constellation Gemini bear their names. And so Castor and Pollux are eternally united in the heavens. But I left Pollux in heaven alone. My Castor did not follow him, because he preferred to remain in Hades and live on there, alone. I too am living on."

Second ending, in the month of June
of the thirty-second year

175

Ego-Clone
Epilogue

The *Blueprint* report is the first clone report from an individual personally involved. Since its appearance, this clone psychobiography has been corroborated in its universal validity for ego-clones. Ego-clone is the term used to label the clone children of the egomaniac, of which Iris Sellin was very typical.

Some of the terms Siri Sellin used for the very first time are part of ordinary usage today. The most important are: *clone-parents*, *clonehood*, and most certainly the word *misbreed*. The words *motwi* and *fatwi* are also slowly coming into use as terms of address for clone-parents.

The first data on psychic health of clone-children are now available for analysis as well. Included are 234 cases in which the clones were older than 15 years of age.

As has been demonstrated by the study, the suicide rate in the sample is only slightly increased over that of normally conceived children (+ 1%). On the other hand, the increased numbers of violent attacks on clone-parents (+ 30%) are striking: Whereas in the group of 10- to 15-year-old *natural kids* (NKs), homicidal acts against fathers and mothers occur so seldom as to say never, in the period surveyed, 30 *clone kids* (CKs) either murdered or attempted to murder their clone-parents in the same period. In these cases the cloning was almost always considered a mitigating circumstance and, as a rule, the CKs underwent long-term psychological treatment by special parentage therapists.

It has already been demonstrated that the success or improvement rate is enormously high. Notably, after the death of a clone-parent, not a few clones establish their own families, in which their offspring are mostly NKs. Instances of a cloned offspring having him- or herself cloned have not yet been observed.

A striking phenomenon is the extremely high intelligence quotient in cloned offspring compared with NKs of the same social and intellectual milieus. Good characteristics as well as bad appear to be intensified. The reasons for this are still unknown.

An interesting hypothesis was offered—almost intuitively, I might say—by Siri Sellin in her *Blueprint* report. She says: The genetic code of a human being stores his life experience; that is, the course of life changes genetic information. It might be that history is also retained on a genetic level, and only the clone receives this credit balance and can pass it on to descendants. Thus the clone-infant—very carefully formulated—would have a more complete genetic provision than either the clone-parent or normally conceived children of the same age for learning and comprehension. On this score too I consider *Blueprint* an interesting document: Perhaps it shows us the typical clone-insight. I find it extremely remarkable that the preceding report was written in this form ten years ago by a very young woman.

Whether a type of life- or personality-memory is actually coded biomedically and on molecular planes and can thus be passed on is still pure speculation. But for centuries it was also unimaginable that anything like a gene might exist or that to a large degree our appearance, our personalities, and our behavior are determined by them. In addition, it is only very recently—in the last century—that science proved we think and feel not with the heart but with the brain, and also that ultimately love or hate are only based on the transmission of electrical and biochemical signals.

Meanwhile, *Blueprint* has become required reading for all men and women who apply for cloning to the the Commission for Reproductive Progress (CRP), which maintains offices in all major cities.

Our experts can grant cloning permission on the basis of the submitted documents if they find them appropriate and sufficient. For medi-clones, of course, firm guidelines exist, and these applications are processed by the medical societies.

To be considered, potential clone-parents must undergo a psychological consultation. The consultation is to determine the degree to which the expectations of the ego-clone are reasonable, that is, if they exceed a healthy norm and thus would clearly result in a case of misbreeding.

According to our current criteria and experience, Iris Sellin would probably have been a borderline case, in which I personally would have agreed to her application for clonehood.

Therefore, I am of course particularly pleased that Siri Sellin has complied with my request and has brought *Blueprint* up-to-date. Ten years after the first version she has supplemented the text with the last chapter, *Pollux Seul*. It shows how much will to live and—I also do not hesitate to say— vital energy resides in the clone Double-Blue, as is usual in most clones: In the end they can, in fact must, develop into survivors. And this makes them remarkably strong.

A fear of societal "clone takeover" is baseless: Clones are on the increase, but they are certainly not overrunning us. In Germany, the number of permissions to duplicate oneself are limited to a maximum 0.32 percent of the national population of reproductive age. This corresponds to the natural birth rate of identical twins. And so it is ensured that the genetic variety intended by nature remains protected.

Clone-conception now takes place in competent government clinics. The costs are not reimbursed by insurance plans.

The CRP has already received 5200 clonehood applications for the next year, half of which have been made by singles, the other half by couples. The numbers have risen steadily since the founding of the CRP, but it will still be decades before the societally permitted clone rate of 0.32 percent is fully reached.

Erika Kneiper, PhD
First president of the CRP
Professor of Human Genetics,
Hildegard von Bingen University,
Hannover, Germany

Author's Afterword

Conceiving and telling a story that is not yet possible means thinking beyond the possible.

The already possible, which provided the very first stimulus for this book, occurred in October 1993. Two American scientists divided human embryos in vitro by "microsurgical methods" and for the first time created "artificial twins." From two- and eight-celled embryos developed two to eight cells with identical genes, which actually continued to develop: the raw material for human clones. The investigators destroyed the embryos at the 32-cell stage and presented their experiment to the public.

What the researchers had done had long been practiced in animal breeding and needed no new findings of any kind. The breaking of the taboo alone was the goal and a signal, a loud warning signal.

Since then, the possible uses for human clones have been considered loudly and shamelessly. For example, clones might be used as future tissue and organ donors, or as "insurance" in case a succeeding child dies. Then the clone twin would be in waiting as a substitute.

There already are some "deferred" twins with identical genes in this world. In several cases, when embryos in vitro have spontaneously divided, doctors froze some of the accidentally occurring "identical" twins. Then, two to three years later, the "frosties" have seen the light of the world and made the acquaintance of their twin sisters or brothers.

What has not yet happened as I write is the cloning of a grown person, to produce twins who are separated by a whole generation like Siri and Iris Sellin, the principal characters in this book.

I was already deep in the middle of work on this story of the future when I was surprised by the story of the sheep Dolly, who was born in 1996 but because of patent issues was not presented to the world until 1997. Dolly was the first mammal that had been successfully cloned, and she came from the udder cells of an adult sheep. Cloned calves and mice swiftly followed, and cloned apes are in the works. The time when human clones will dwell among us has come much closer.

"When do you think the first cloned human will be born?" asked the news magazine *Der Spiegel* of the American molecular biologist Lee Silver in the summer of 1998. The author of the book *Remaking Eden: Cloning and Beyond in a Brave New World* replied: "When the news of sheep clone Dolly flashed around the world, I thought, in ten years. Now I think, in five years."

When *Blueprint* first went to press, in December of 1998, the world was hearing the news of Dr. Lee Bo Yeon of Korea, who had removed the nucleus from the egg cell of a thirty-year-old woman and transplanted the genes from a body cell of the same woman to the egg cell. When a human clone actually developed, the doctor from Seoul is said to have "voluntarily" discontinued the experiment. Once again, the breaking of the taboo had been the sole goal, an act that made the doctor famous throughout the world. And from that moment it has been established beyond doubt: What was done to Dolly could also be done to humans.

I have no illusions: Researchers will clone humans, and humans will have themselves cloned. The clone is already living among us, if still only in thoughts and words, films and books.

Dolly and her animal successors are mute. So an article about these animal clone attempts bears a title that is appropriate, "The Silence of the Lambs"—in reference to the well-known psychothriller. But human clones can speak, can tell about themselves—like Siri Sellin, who tells of her clone existence and consciousness in *Blueprint*.

I was encouraged to write this book by the many adults and young people who read my first future history, *Geboren 1999* [Born 1999], and their positive reactions. Young people in particular as future investigators, consumers, or research subjects have very often and eagerly discussed *their* possible future and often asked me to write a "continuation" some day.

Blueprint is not a continuation of *Geboren 1999*, but both books do have something in common: They tell what the use of scientific information can mean for an individual person, what "progress" can do to and in someone.

As early as the beginning of the eighties, in the essay "Let's Clone a Human: Reflections on the Prospect of Genetic Experiments with Ourselves," philosopher Hans Jonas declared, "The animal breeder *knows* what qualities he is looking for in an animal every time." And Jonas goes on to ask, "But do we, too, know what we want in a human being?"

A worldwide prohibition against cloning humans was demanded and discussed. But what has actually been *done* against human cloning to date? Very little!

General references to naturalness and human dignity or to old biological laws leave us rather helpless. Cloning will without doubt "establish a hitherto unknown type of interpersonal relationship between genetic prototypes and copies," writes the Frankfurt philosopher Jürgen Habermas. "As far as I can see, the cloning of humans must damage every condition of symmetry in the relationship of grown persons with one another, on which formerly rested the idea of mutual respect of equal freedom."

What personal and societal morality means in the case of cloning must be discussed further. And what it means to have the courage to be moral must also be argued in individual cases.

Blueprint is a book for argument.

Charlotte Kerner
Lübeck, September 1998

Sources and Acknowledgments

A great help to me in understanding the clone theme was the Hans Jonas essay mentioned in the Afterword: "Let's Clone a Human" (in German), in *Technik, Medizin und Ethik. Zur Praxis des Prinzips Verantwortung* (Frankfurt: suhrkamp taschenbuch, 1987); and the book by Claus Koch: *The End of Naturalness: A Treatise on Biotechnology and Bioethics* (in German) (Munich, 1994).

I have also gained ideas from Dieter E. Zimmer: "The Human and His Double: About Twins and Twin Research" (in German), in *Experimente des Lebens* (Munich: Heyne-Sachbuch, 1993).

Finally, for the most recent state of the discussion, I used a series of ethical debates in *Der Zeit* (February/March 1998) with contributions from Dieter E. Zimmer, Jürgen Habermas, and Reinhard Merkel and the outstanding book by Gina Kolata: *Clone: The Road to Dolly, and the Path Ahead* (New York: William Morrow, 1998).

The passages on twin mythology are based on three publications: Tobias Angert: "Lisa and Lottie or Two

Personalities? (in German), in *Forschung Frankfurt*, vol. 9, no. 1, 1991; Rainer Jehl, Roswitha Terlinden (eds.): "Artist Twins," Exhibition Catalogue, Symposium (Irsee, Germany: Schwabenakademie Irsee, 1994; Karin Schlieben-Troschke: *Psychology of the Twin Personality* (in German) (Cologne, 1981).

For Siri Sellin's art I have taken as a model the works of artist Rebecca Horn. The speech of the gallery owner and the explanation of Siri Sellin on pages 169ff. are based on a speech from Nationalgalerie Berlin, Kunsthalle Wien in cooperation with Guggenheim Museum (ed): *Rebecca Horn* (New York, 1994). Rebecca Horn's work of art *La lune seule*, which I was able to see and study at an exhibition in Berlin in 1994, is the model for the installation *Pollux seul* (pp. 173 ff.).

The color photograph *Chicago Bulls* is by Christine Hohenbüchler.

Through talks and literary references, family therapist and medical psychology professor Dr. Friedrich Balck, Lübeck/ University of Dresden, and biologist and twin researcher Dr. Tobias Angert, University of Frankfurt am Main, have helped to bring about my better understanding of the relationship of the clones, those twins of the future.

I owe very great thanks to the Rumanian-born composer Violeta Dinescu, Professor of Applied Composition at the Carl von Ossietsky University, Oldenburg. She has taken much time to talk with me and has provided me with insights into her work. Her impressive music, which she made available to me on cassettes and videos—from *Dewdrops* to the children's opera *The 35th of May*—I was kindly permitted to ascribe to Iris Sellin. A catalogue with a complete listing of Violeta Dinescu's work is available from: contemporary music Adesso, CH-6958 Corticiasca, Switzerland (Tel./Fax 0041 91 944 1326)

Discography (Selected):

"Mein Haus ein Stein" [My House a Stone], *Trio Contraste*, LC 0504 VTCD (This CD contains eight of Dinescu's works, including *Echoes I* and *II*.)

"Tautropfen" [Dewdrops], published by GEDOK, Heidelberg

"Cime lointaine" on: *Mattias Arter, Oboe Solo* from Adesso, pan Classics 510 087

"Echoes I" on: *D'un matin de printemps*. Bayer Records BR 100169

"Wenn der freude tränen fliessen" [When tears of joy flow] on: *On and off the keys*. VMM Vienna Modern Masters 2027

"Es nimmt mich wunder..." on: *Urla Kahl, Horn*. Salto Records International SAL 7001

My editor Susanne Härtel was, as always, a very important and productive critic and companion on the long path to the finished book.

About the Author Charlotte Kerner is an award-winning journalist in her native Germany and writes regularly on medical subjects. She was awarded the German Youth Literature prize in 1997.

About the Translator Elizabeth D. Crawford has won many awards for her translations, including the prestigious Batchelder Award as well as a Batchelder Honor. She lives in Orange, Connecticut.

Cover photograph copyright© 2000 by Bruce Berg/Visuals Unlimited

Cover design by Zachary Marell